Achilles' Rage

The WARRIORS Series

Vol. 1

A Novel by Lee Smyth

www.LeeSmyth.com
AUTHOR: Lee Smyth
SERIES: The WARRIORS Series, Volume 1
TITLE: Achilles' Rage
ISBN-13: 978-1539352204
ISBN-10: 153935220X

For Lee's latest novels, go to **www.LeeSmyth.com**

Books in the **Take-It-to-the-*MAX*** series for video-game fanatics can be read in any order, but the following sequence is recommended: 1. MAX RoW (<u>R</u>ighters <u>o</u>f <u>W</u>rongs), 2. MAX CoW (<u>C</u>razies <u>o</u>f <u>W</u>ahoo), 3. MAX WoW (<u>W</u>orld <u>o</u>f <u>W</u>heels), 4. MAX PoW (<u>P</u>rom <u>o</u>f <u>W</u>ahoo).

In the **GoG series (Gods of Games)** for video-game addicts, *Total Control* and *Total O.P.M.* are for teens and are best when read in that order. *Total Catastrophe, Totally Unleashed*, and *Total Chaos* can be read in any order and are recommended for both <u>middle schoolers & teens</u>. <u>Animal lovers</u> will LOVE *Totally Unleashed* and *Total Catastrophe* (which is also known as "Total Cat").

Books in the **WARRIORS** series can be read in any order: 1. Achilles' Rage, 2. Tel's Odyssey, 3. Hercules' Pain.

Books in the **Mac and Dekker** series ("James Bond" for a new generation of readers) can be read in any order, but the following sequence is recommended: 1. Midas, 2. Shoot the Moon, 3. (planned) The Big Bang.

Books in the **Re-Imagined** series can be read in any order: 1. Treasure Island (a re-imagining of Robert Louis Stevenson's Treasure Island), 2. Frankenstein, My Father (a re-imagining of Mary Shelley's Frankenstein), 3. White Scar, the Ship Wrecker (a re-imagining of Herman Melville's Moby Dick).

OTHER NOVELS for teens by Lee Smyth: 1. Rev Willie, A Voodoo-Hoodoo Gumbo, With Blood (And Laughs), 2. Damaged, 3. Filthy Rich + Dirt Poor. For details, see **www.LeeSmyth.com**

TABLE OF CONTENTS

CONTENTS

Foreword

Achilles and Hector, the two greatest warriors of all time, have been famous for 2,500 years.

Twenty-five hundred years – wow!

Most rock stars and football heroes are forgotten after a quarter of a century, but everyone from your great grandfather to your little sister has heard about the half-god Achilles, a prince named Hector, the wooden Trojan horse that ended the war, and the woman who started it, Helen of Troy.

This novel was inspired by The Iliad. The author has written the tale that he *wishes* Homer had told rather than translating 15,693 lines of Greek poetry. For those of you who want to read a word-for-word retelling, consider translations by Stanley Lombardo (clear, modern language), Robert Fagles (elegant prose), or Richard Lattimore (poetry).

The old blind poet wasn't always faithful to the myths; sometimes he just winged it and changed details. The author admits that he has occasionally done the same thing:

A well told tale triumphs over a thousand tiring truths.

CHAPTER 1: I know it's wrong.

NARRATOR: JEM

I look both ways then steal two bucketfuls from the others. I know it's wrong, but nothing about the past few days has been fair or right.

Nothing.

Beauty looks at me and I see the panic in her eyes. Perhaps she sees the fear in mine too. I'm beginning to realize that Wren and I may never see our home or our mother again.

Home is Lemnos, an island where both the Greeks and Trojans used to trade freely with us. Dad got "recruited" to fight in the war three years ago. And now he's dead.

We're next.

Sixteen is supposed to be the official age when someone can be drafted to fight. Wren, my twin sister, and I are barely eleven, but King Agamemnon is desperate for new soldiers, stable hands, and slaves.

I quickly dump the stolen oats into the feeding troughs in front of Beauty, Brazen, Black, and Bold. These horses used to be ours. Now they belong to the Greek army.

Beauty and Brazen have already devoured their rations. Their eyes beg me for more.

"I know it's not enough. I'm hungry too," I whisper to Beauty, then shudder as I notice the raw marks above Brazen's front legs. The leather straps that keep him from falling when this huge ship is rocked by the waves have also cut into his flesh. He's lost ten pounds, probably more, during the four days we've been on board.

The light above the hatch door is blocked as someone leans over it. I cringe, knowing that if Scarp catches me stealing oats for our horses again, he'll beat me. The last thing I want to do is give him another opportunity to kill me.

"Hurry, we're docking!" Wren says.

They're not yours anymore. That's what Scarp yelled at me yesterday.

Tell it to them, I said, pointing at our four horses. That's when he added a few blows to my back that raised welts.

As I rush toward the ladder, something incredibly valuable catches my eye – two eggs.

There's a chicken cage near the horse stalls, but its latch is broken. So now the six loose chickens spend all day driving the pigs crazy.

I grab the eggs and rush back toward our horses. I crack the first shell on a wooden post, carefully empty its contents into my cupped left hand, and feed it to Brazen.

"Say strong," I say. "I'll find you a stable soon."

Beauty's lost almost as much weight as Brazen has, so the second egg is hers.

"I won't let them hurt you," I promise.

I watched Ukiah the Claw beat two of our other horses to force them up the ramp onto another ship. I'm praying they're still alive.

Scarp and the Claw stole twenty horses from our stables. The only four that I'm sure are safe are the ones in front of me.

Three of the more than thirty people crammed onto this two-mast ship have died. No prayers, no ceremonies – Scarp just dumped them overboard along with the garbage.

* * *

"Wow, do you stink," Wren whispers as I join her at the railings.

"Look who's talking," I say with an arched eyebrow. Both of us were in our muck-raking clothes when Scarp's men grabbed us.

But in a way, that was lucky. We were assigned to the "stables" in the belly of this ship.

As a breeze blows the morning mist away, Wren's eyes grow with amazement. "There are *hundreds* of ships on shore."

I squint to make out more details. "And thousands of soldiers."

Everywhere I look, I see tree stumps, bonfires, and tents. What used to be a forest is now a small city, all of it created by the invaders, the Greek army.

Wren is shivering. Wordlessly, I put my arm around her and pull her closer. Winter is coming soon and we've got to help each other survive. No one else will because no one else who cares is alive.

That's what I'm afraid of anyway.

Old memories stir inside me as I stare at the hillside. "Dad talked about this place. He visited here before the war."

Doubt is written all over Wren's face. After all, our father has been dead for almost three years.

I point at the fortress on the top of the hill. "*Walls that never end* – that's what he said."

They seem huge even from here. And they surround the hillside. No wonder this war has been going on for so long.

"This must be Troy," I say. "It has to be."

"Then this," Wren trembles, "is where Dad died."

Two crew members are approaching, so we stop talking. The one who's about sixteen is Jake, one of the few guys working for Scarp who doesn't treat us like cattle.

"Jake, what's that smell?" a sailor even younger than me asks. "What are they burning?"

"Bodies."

The boy sees he's serious. "You mean people?"

Jake nods.

The wind has shifted and is blowing smoke in our direction. Two huge bonfires are burning, one near us on the eastern shore, the other on the west, where very few tents are located.

"Why don't they bury them," the kid asks, "and put their names on the graves?"

"Because there's no place left to put 'em. Every day, our soldiers slaughter the Trojans and they slaughter us. And there's been a lot of ...

sickness. If you're going on shore later, stay away from the corpses. You see those fires?"

"They're huge," the kid says.

"The one closest to us is a funeral pyre for the soldiers."

"The ones who died in battle?"

Jake nods.

The boy turns his attention to an even larger mound next to the fire on the west end. "And that pile, all of it's ... ?"

Jake hesitates. "More dead people."

The stack is twice as high as a man. The slaves throwing the corpses into the fire are wearing rags over their noses and mouths.

"But there's no blood."

"Swords didn't kill 'em," Jake says.

The kid lowers his voice. "The plague?"

Jake nods. "I saw 'em hauling fifty a day out of the forced-labor camp before we sailed for Lemnos."

"It's spreading?" the kid asks.

"Definitely." Jake sighs. "Some of the soldiers say we've been cursed by one of Apollo's holy men. King Agamemnon claimed a priest's daughter as a war prize. They say he grabbed her while she was on her knees *in* the temple."

"Is it true?"

"I don't know nothin' but what my own eyes tell me, and every day I see two things. We're losing. And a lot of good men are dying for no good reason."

"All hands on deck! Prepare for docking," shouts Scarp, a brute of a man with greasy black hair and nothing but brown stumps left for teeth.

"Quick, downstairs," I say to Wren.

She hesitates. "If you make him angry – "

"He's busy on the forward deck. And if anyone asks why we're with the horses, say *Scarp assigned us to the stables.*"

"Okay, good," Wren says.

I raise my voice as much as I dare. "No! Say it like you're pissed."

Her eyes widen. It's not a word I use often.

"Say it!"

"Scarp assigned us to the stables!"

"That's better," I say. "Let's go."

CHAPTER 2: "*That* one."

NARRATOR: WREN

Thud!

"What was that?" I say to Jem.

"The anchor, I think."

The cargo hold's massive door creaks open, a long ramp is lowered, and air that's actually breathable finally arrives below deck.

Then someone shimmies down one of the masts to our level. I back into the shadows.

"Act like you belong here," Jem whispers.

He needs to follow his own advice.

Jake lands on a pile of hay, sees us, and smiles. "Pigs don't kick," he says as he grabs a pole and starts prodding them onto the ramp. "That's why I'd love it if you'd handle the horses."

Jem nods but he looks like he might hurl. I can't blame him; we need a lot of good luck during the next few minutes or we'll be in one of the forced labor camps by nightfall.

As I guide Brazen and Beauty toward the narrow ramp, Brazen snorts and rears onto his hind legs. The water has spooked him.

A broad-shouldered man on the unloading dock turns and stares. He's angry. The last thing I wanted to do was attract attention.

I throw a blanket over Brazen's eyes and whisper, "Trust me, big guy," then guide him down the ramp. Beauty is following behind me. Jem is leading Black and Bold.

I squint as my eyes adjust from the dark of the cargo hold to the brightness on the dock.

"Scarp assigned us to the stables!" I say to the barrel-chested man.

I'm not sure if he's going to spit in my face or toss me into the bay.

Jake's ten steps away and he saves us. "The stable master is expecting those four horses, so get moving." He glances toward the west and says, "Go to the black banner."

After reaching the shoreline, Jem and I exchange glances. Never before have I seen such relief in my twin's eyes.

We merge into the chaos that surrounds us. Four other cargo ships landed at the same time that ours did and all are being unloaded.

Behind us I hear a man's voice that seems to float above the others.

"Send the pigs to my campsite."

A soldier replies, "Odysseus told us to distribute them equally."

"And I'm telling you that if you wish to live another day, you will obey my orders."

"Yes, my lord."

I continue toward the black banners, hoping to put as much distance as possible between us and this horrible man. One word from him and our horses will be his.

"Which ship contains my war prizes?" the big-voiced man asks.

A soldier points. "It's unloading now, my lord."

Jem and I stare in amazement. Everyone walking from the cargo hold is a girl or young woman.

"This is a sorry lot you've brought me. There's barely a maiden among them."

"I've done my best, sire."

"You'll do better or you'll pay the consequences."

Finally I gain the courage to glance at this powerful man with a big voice and an even larger appetite. I'm shocked.

Jem and I have seen extraordinarily wealthy traders in the bazaar on Lemnos, but nothing like this. The man is fat beyond what my imagination thought was possible. And he's wearing animal skins so plush and rare that I have no idea what they're called.

He's seated on an elevated couch that's being carried by six warriors. They've lifted him so that he's four feet higher than the tallest man among us.

In the distance, double gates are opened. Wagon after wagon enters. Some are filled with dead men still wearing battle armor. Others contain bloodied soldiers who are screaming in pain.

An olive-skinned girl carrying two baskets filled with herbs is hurrying alongside one of the wagons, pressing bandages against gaping wounds. She's unflinching, braver than I could ever be.

Some of the men are begging for a quick death. But the fat man is unmoved.

"*That* one," he says, pointing at the girl with the herbs. "She'll warm my bed tonight."

"She's part of the Spartan camp, sir. There may be trouble."

"You heard me. Find out her name."

When the heavy man and his guards are far past us, I decide it's safe to talk again.

"You remember what Jake said about the banner?"

"Yeah," Jem says. "It's black. So?"

"That's Achilles' color."

Jem slows his pace but says nothing.

At home, we often went with Dad whenever he had extra horses to sell in the central market. Half of the traders were from other countries and some of them barely spoke a word of Greek. But all of them, no exceptions, knew that name.

Achilles.

Most of the stories we heard about him were crazy - stuff no one, perhaps not even a god, could do. Even so, we loved hearing them.

"And he's a Spartan," I say to Jem. Every school boy in Greece knows the Spartan colors: blood-red and black.

"All their warriors look the same," he says.

I nod. "Huge. And hard. They don't talk much either."

"So we wouldn't know him even if we saw him."

"Maybe," I admit, "maybe not. Except that he's godlike."

"You know any gods?" Jem asks sarcastically.

I shake my head, then re-focus on our destination: the tents under the black banners.

A regiment of Spartan warriors marches past us. Black banners, black tunics. They're dressed as if the temperature is twenty degrees warmer. Many of the men are injured, but all are marching as if they feel no pain.

I'm staring in wonder, then see something that makes me look away.

"How's that possible?" I ask.

Jem, too, is stunned. The sight was sickening.

"I've never seen that many scars," he says.

"Or that much blood."

He nods. "How could anyone get wounded that many times and still be alive?"

I shake my head, as bewildered as Jem is. Then I realize the answer to my own question.

You'd have to be godlike.

As we move closer to the pennants, I realize that we've made a mistake.

"These flags aren't black."

I see the tension in Jem's face as he realizes I'm right.

"They look darker because they're gritty from all of the smoke."

I nod. "Dark blue, that's what, Ithaca?" All of the poets and storytellers call that color midnight-blue.

"It doesn't matter whose horses we help with," Jem says. "We started working in Dad's stable when we were four. Wren, we can do this!"

I take a deep breath and nod. I'm trying not to think about the forced labor camps.

"Beautiful horses," says a soldier, "but they could certainly use a good meal."

I jump, startled to realize that he was so close behind us, but there's no meanness in his voice. He's older than most of the soldiers we've seen, about Dad's age.

As he dismounts from a dappled mare, I notice a long jagged scar on the inside of his left thigh. His armor is heavily gouged and splattered with blood, but he's not seriously injured. His sword and shield are expertly made, something

I'd expect to be owned by someone wealthy, perhaps even a king, but nothing about him makes me think that he wants to be treated as a nobleman.

"Scarp assigned us to the stables!" Jem blurts out. He's panicking.

The soldier glances at Jem, then at me. "Did he really?" His eyes are laughing at us.

"The Spartan stables," Jem adds.

"No, Ithaca," I say. "I think he said Ithaca."

"You're both lousy liars," he says with a large grin, "but that's something I can help you with."

I'm stunned. I have no idea what to say.

He expertly unbridles his horse, then says, "Scarp sends the small and the weak to the forced labor camp. Then he starves them and works them to death."

"We're good with horses." I'm almost begging. "Our father owned a stable."

He tosses me the bridle. "Yeah? Let's see what you can do."

I clap my hands twice. "Beauty, come here."

The man shakes his head and points at Brazen. "No, the skittish one."

I stand on my toes, then whisper into our fastest horse's ear. "Easy, boy, easy." I reach up and rub his neck with the palm of my left hand, then touch his nose.

Hoping for a carrot, he opens his mouth. I slip the bit between his teeth, then pull the bridle over his ears. Brazen's eyes show his surprise but he doesn't fight me.

"Well done," the man says.

"Thank you." My words are barely audible.

"You're clever. And gutsy. I like that. I'm Odysseus and you're welcome in my camp. You'll be safe there, I promise you."

I believe him.

"O-dis-ee-us?" Jem says, struggling with his name.

"Even my wife calls me Ody. And you are?"

"Wren," I say.

Ody shifts his glance to my brother.

"Jem."

"Where is your home?"

Jem kicks at the sandy soil. "Lemnos."

"So it's come to this, has it?" Ody sighs. "Scarp now steals children from an island that has never harmed Greece in any way. Then he calls them volunteers. May the gods grant that bastard a slow and painful death."

Someone nearby laughs.

We look up and see a brown-skinned servant woman who's washing clothes outside a tent. Embarrassed, she covers her mouth, then bows.

"Dysendra, you know you don't have to kneel for me." He smiles, then adds, "I need your help, please."

As the woman approaches, I see that she's dressed in layer after layer of what my mother would call rags.

"Take these two to the scrubbing area, find them some clothes, and protect them as if they were your own. They'll eat at my campsite tonight."

She nods, then hesitates before adding, "You've forgotten the King's Council, sir."

Ody shakes his head. "The heralds' horns were loud enough. I'm tired of Agamemnon's lies and have better things to do." Then he bends onto one knee and looks me in the eye. "Please trust me with your horses."

Even though Ody joked just moments ago that he's a skillful liar, I can see through his eyes into his soul. He reminds me of my dad.

I hand him the reins, surrendering the only things of value we have left, the only treasures we truly love.

Dysendra bows again to Ody, this time even lower than the first.

As Ody leaves, Dysendra whispers to us, "For King Agamemnon, I kneel because I must. For Ody, I bow to show my respect."

She begins walking rapidly as if she's a woman with a purpose in life, not a slave. As we pass a bewildering maze of tents, Dysendra glances at each of us.

"Have you been sick?"

"No," I answer.

"You're just skinny?"

Jem nods.

"Good. There has been far too much death here."

She turns to Jem and asks, "How long since your last full meal?"

"Four days," he says.

"Scarp!" She spits as if the man's name has left a bitter taste in her mouth.

On a nearby pathway we see a downed mule with yellow mucous drooling from its open mouth. Saddle bags are still attached to its back. It looks as if he dropped dead in mid-step.

"Lord Agamemnon likes temple girls," Dysendra comments, "so the high priest cursed our mules. Now we're breaking the backs of our best horses with loads they used to carry."

We pass several tents overflowing with sick men. The smell is so bad that Jem and I use our filthy shirts to cover our noses.

"Plague rot," Dysendra explains. "There's nothing that can be done for them. It starts with unending thirst, then a rash and days of black vomit. The retching doesn't end even after they're stick-thin."

Soon we arrive at an area filled with boiling laundry cauldrons. Without a word, an old woman sticks her hands into my hair.

"I do not have lice!" I complain loudly.

She tightens her grip on my head, finishes inspecting me, and pushes me aside. Jem endures the same treatment.

"I'll get you some clothes," Dysendra says, then points at a pot that's overflowing with bloody froth. "Everything you're wearing goes in there."

A man with a stump for a leg points Jem toward one curtain, me to another. I'm grateful that we're given plenty of hot water to remove the stench of Scarp's hellhole.

Finally we're allowed to dress. The tunics and leggings that Dysendra has found for us are too big and have reddish spots all over them, but I no longer care about such things. There's no doubt in my mind that the stains are from blood splatters.

Jem and I are clean, dry, warm, and, most important, safe. Everyone else in our village is now either dead or a slave. It feels only slightly odd that we're alive because we lied: *Scarp assigned us to the stables*.

Our noses know we're nearing the cook's pavilion long before we arrive. Breakfast ended hours ago, but Dysendra's smiling face gains us entry to anywhere we want to go inside the Spartan or Ithacan camps.

Rabbits are roasting on spits. Carrot and potato stew is boiling inside huge kettles supported by copper tripods. Hurried preparations for lunch are already underway, but every cook and servant finds time to sneak a few goodies to us. We're ravenously hungry, so even their scraps seem like a feast.

As we return to Ody's encampment, we pass a clearing filled with hundreds of men. Dysendra stops abruptly, then places a

finger to her lips. "King Agamemnon,"
she whispers.

It's the horrible fat man we saw earlier
this morning.

CHAPTER 3: "Her protector is Achilles."

NARRATOR: WREN

Jem's eyes are growing wider. King Agamemnon is guarded by fifty of the most heavily armored warriors I've ever seen. A thin, pale girl is trembling at his feet. Her legs and arms are tied with strips of leather.

The guards recognize Dysendra and allow us to creep closer.

"Apollo's vestal virgins are sacred!" says a gray-bearded high priest in a long robe that extends to his ankles.

Agamemnon snarls. "Hold your tongue or I'll have it cut out!"

The high priest's assistant leaps to his feet. "And then the plague will wipe you from these shores, you and the filthy degenerates you brought with - "

Agamemnon points at the young man's throat. A guard responds instantly. Mid-sentence, the assistant's words end and his screams begin.

The sharp blade of a long spear has been thrust into his neck but not yet removed. Agamemnon twists his right wrist and the silent command is obeyed: the bronze blade snaps the assistant's jawbone, then splits his tongue. His body falls to the ground.

Even the grossest excesses are barely enough for this man who calls himself our king of kings.

An old man in royal robes who's alarmed by these actions rushes to Agamemnon's side.

"Nestor," Dysendra whispers. "He was once our supreme leader."

"I beg of you, king of kings," Nestor says softly, "the high priest has suffered enough. As has his daughter."

The high priest, wearing an orange and yellow robe that shimmers like the sun, is kneeling next to the trembling girl.

The veins in Agamemnon's thick neck are throbbing. He lifts a wooden staff that's decorated with hundreds of ribbons and rare feathers, then pounds its base on a tree stump. "I claimed her as a war prize, as was my right."

"And you brought the plague upon us all," a soldier mutters.

Agamemnon's angry eyes are searching the crowd, looking for the man who dared to speak. He's somewhere within a group of a hundred other warriors, none of whom betray him.

"She's a *priest's* daughter!" shouts one of his companions.

Nestor glances at the soldiers and says, "I ask for your silence for a few moments."

Every legionnaire stands at attention. Nestor continues.

"This man – Apollo's highest prophet – has not just humbled himself before us, he has also offered compensation that should not be quickly dismissed."

Nestor removes a silk scarf that's covering a chest overflowing with riches. Many, myself included, gasp.

"Persian gold," he says, "Egyptian sapphires, and Mycenaean silver!"

Agamemnon glances at the offering, snarls, and looks away.

Nestor turns to face the high priest and asks, "If our king of kings accepts your generous gift and returns your daughter, will you pray for an end to this plague that has taken so many from us?"

The priest nods.

"Accept the offering. Accept the offering," some soldiers chant.

Agamemnon hurls an ivory-handled knife into the heart of one of the offending men. Blood bubbles through the wound, he falls.

The chanting ends.

The king gulps wine from a silver goblet, then throws the dregs into the captive girl's face.

"Remove this filthy bitch from my sight."

Dysendra is stunned. Jem and I exchange glances. We're astonished that this is Lord Agamemnon's way of accepting the high priest's offering.

How can this pig of a man be a king? Discontented murmurings are heard everywhere.

Guards place the gilded chest at Agamemnon's feet and escort the girl back to her father.

Agamemnon turns to the former king of kings, old Nestor.

"I have the right to compensation. Surely you cannot argue with me on that point?"

Nestor lowers his head and backs away.

"Good," Agamemnon mutters, then turns to one of his lieutenants. "Who's the girl I saw this morning, the one with the herbs?"

"Briseis."

A regiment of a hundred Spartans stiffens.

Nestor moves cautiously toward Agamemnon. "Her protector is Achilles."

The so-called king of kings laughs, then drunkenly bellows, "I claim Briseis as my prize."

* * *

The king's council is over, but it's impossible to stop thinking about what just occurred.

"Why," I ask Lysendra, "does Ody obey that man's commands?"

"Because he has no choice."

Jem's face hardens.

"You don't believe me, do you?" Dysendra asks.

Jem says nothing.

"Agamemnon is a cruel king but not a stupid one. He finds out who every man cares about most. Then he threatens to crush those people under his heel."

Dysendra pauses to make sure that no one is near enough to overhear what she's about to tell us.

"Ody has a wife, Penelope, whom he loves boundlessly. And a son."

Jem gulps. "A son?"

"Yes, about your age."

Dysendra imitates Agamemnon's growling voice. *"Your wife and child will die unexpectedly if you refuse to fight for me."*

We walk silently until we reach the area outside the stables. Dark blue pennants fly above us.

I peek inside the horse stalls and see Black, Brazen, Bold, and Beauty feeding from an oat-filled trough. I'm about to go inside when I hear a shout from inside a nearby tent.

"Call for them!"

The man who's screaming those words is in great pain.

Tent flaps are thrown open and soldiers wearing black and blood-red tunics rush out. That's when I realize that just a simple dirt pathway separates us from the Spartan camp.

Inside the large tent I see a skeleton of a lion leaping to make a kill, a bed supported by large bones, animal skins for blankets, an open chest containing black armor, and a man so heavily scarred that his skin no longer resembles flesh.

Jem's eyes widen. "Achilles?"

Dysendra nods.

"Call for them *now!*" Achilles shouts.

The gash in his thigh is cut to the bone.

A huge warrior emerges from the tent, and inhales deeply.

Dysendra covers her ears and mouths the man's name: *Ajax*.

"Briseis! Patroclus!" he roars.

The voice is as large as the man. His chest is the size of a giant redwood tree. He's still wearing his battle armor, which is splattered with the blood of his enemies.

At least half of this enormous tent city has surely heard Ajax's call. Briseis, who's only a year or two older than I am, comes running. She's carrying a basket that's overflowing with herbs and tiny pottery urns.

Unflinching, she stares at Achilles' wound, grabs an orange pot from her bag, then a black jar. Next she coats her palms with the gooey ointments from both.

"This will sting," she warns him.

Achilles tenses his body, then shudders as this tiny, olive-skinned girl coats the edges of his wound.

I glance at Dysendra, hoping for an explanation.

"Wild yarrow," she whispers. "It clots the blood. Poppy extract blunts the pain."

Jem's wrinkled forehead shows his confusion. "But Achilles' mother was a goddess. He's immortal, isn't he?"

"He feels the pain just like you or me," Dysendra says, "but no matter the wound, he always heals."

Kicked to the side of his bed is Achilles' bloodied thigh protector. The leather strap that holds the back and front pieces together looks as if it's been severed by another man's sword.

From a hundred steps away, I hear the sound of running feet. The Spartan warriors outside Achilles' tent murmur the new arrival's name:

"Patroclus."

I crane my neck and see a handsome young man whose blonde curls are bouncing as he runs. He's clutching a rolled leopard skin under his right arm.

Panting heavily, Patroclus enters Achilles' tent. He glances at the deep wound and bites his lip. Tears well in his eyes.

"Damn the Trojan bastard who did this to you!"

Patroclus unrolls his animal skin, revealing the tools of his trade: scalpels for cutting, ivory-tusk needles for sewing, and cat gut for stitching the wound.

Ever so gently, Patroclus touches Achilles' forehead. He opens his eyes.

"Ready?"

Achilles tightens his horribly scarred hands onto the sides of his bed. That's when I notice that the bed posts and supports are made from the thigh bones of elephants.

Patroclus begins closing the wound as the marching feet of at least fifty men thunder toward us on a cobblestone roadway.

"Fetch the bitch."

I recognize the voice: King Agamemnon.

He's leaning back against his elevated couch, which is silk-covered. Six guards are holding a horizontal pole on their left shoulders. Six more are supporting another oak pole on their right.

Even the giant Ajax must look up to gaze at the high and mighty pig-man.

The king's herald enters Achilles' tent without asking for permission. He's holding a royal scepter that's seven-feet high.

At the top of the pole is an elaborately carved three-headed dog. It's Cerberus, the hound that guards the gates of Hades. Black fur, glowing red eyes, a mane of snakes, and a lion's claws – the gruesomely detailed carving itself is enough to make many lower their eyes.

The herald plunges the scepter's sharpened point into the ground with impressive force. "All hail the king of kings!"

Agamemnon enters. "I claim the girl as my war prize."

Patroclus refocuses his eyes on Agamemnon and stares in disbelief. "She's needed here."

Old Nestor hobbles to Agamemnon's side and whispers, "You'll gain a girl and lose the war."

The king of kings sneers contemptuously. "Achilles I cannot kill. You I can. Never forget that."

Nestor bows his head and retreats. Agamemnon turns to a guard and points at Briseis.

"Make her grovel before me."

A heartbeat later, Briseis' face and the shoulders of her deerskin dress have been forced into the dirt.

With shocking suddenness, Achilles' bed crashes to the ground. One of its elephant-thigh supports is now in Achilles' hands.

Wham!

The huge club strikes the guard's helmet, crushing one side. He falls and blood streams from his head.

Crack!

The elephant bone connects with the herald's hip. He releases the scepter as he crumples to the ground.

Achilles is now holding the seven-foot pole as if it's a spear. The sharpened end is pointed at Agamemnon's heart.

"I cannot promise," Achilles says, "that I will not kill the next man who touches this girl."

"Think twice about murdering a king," Agamemnon snarls.

"And what, oh king of kings, would be my punishment?" Achilles asks defiantly. "To fight another year in this plague-cursed war?!"

Agamemnon shifts his eyes to the blood flowing down Achilles' thigh but he says nothing.

Angry, Achilles continues. He's almost spitting out the words as a crowd of Spartans grows.

"The piles of corpses are growing faster than we can burn them. Yet the fool we are forced to call our *king* spends his days in search of new whores and more wine. Now he demands that a mere child warm his bed." Achilles points at Briseis, who's trembling, and says, "This girl, who finds the herbs that soothe our wounds, is no one's whore, and she will *never* be yours."

Achilles' voice remains strong but his face is growing pale. I'm shocked that

any man can lose this much blood and
still be alive.

"Soon enough," Agamemnon bellows to the
soldiers, "each of you will have more
Trojan gold than you can carry; all will
share glory!"

"Glory?!" Achilles shouts. "We sleep in
tents and shiver throughout the night.
Each day, we stand in mud so that we can
slaughter other men who have never
wronged us. No Trojan ever stole our
cattle or salted our fields. This is a
war of greed, and it is *your* battle, not
ours!"

Agamemnon sneers at Achilles as if he's
talking to a child having a temper
tantrum.

"Kings write the final chronicles, and
my scribes will call you what I command
them to: *Achilles the Coward*. Hector the
Trojan will then go down in history as
the greatest warrior of all time, not
you. And remember this well: all tribal
leaders – including your father – signed
the same pledge to fight common enemies.
Those who dishonor it will pay a heavy
price."

Achilles is seething with anger. "As *we* fight, *you* plunder innocent villages. I will no longer obey the orders of a man who claims young girls as war prizes." He lifts the heavy pole high above his head and shouts, "I swear by this scepter that I will not return to battle until you release Briseis, untouched."

Achilles collapses. The scepter rolls from his hand, but he's still conscious.

Agamemnon turns to his guards. "Bring the girl. If she fights you, beat her."

Briseis' eyes are filled with panic. As the guards drag her away, she screams to Achilles. "My sisters were taken this morning!"

"Who?!" Achilles asks weakly.

Briseis is able to get three words past the gag that's being forced into her mouth:

"Scarp and Ukiah!"

As Patroclus repeats their names, his voice is filled with disgust. "Scarp the Defiler and Ukiah the Claw — the scum from Xanthium Prison."

Achilles' face hardens. "They will die screaming. This I swear upon the sacred River Styx."

Dysendra's eyes widen as Achilles utters the unbreakable oath. Zeus himself is bound by those words.

As Achilles' eyes close, his breathing slows. Seconds later, the pulse in his neck is almost undetectable.

Alarmed, I shout. "Patroclus, he's dying!"

CHAPTER 4: "Some called it murder. It wasn't."

NARRATOR: JEM

"Patroclus, he's dying!" Wren shouts.

"No, this is normal. He goes into a deep, deep sleep and can't be awakened. Tomorrow morning, he'll open his eyes, eat ravenously – and want revenge."

Patroclus isn't even looking at Achilles. He's concentrating on threading cat gut through an ivory needle.

The sharpened point punctures the long wound on Achilles' thigh but there's not even the slightest reaction from him.

I look away. "How's it possible ... ?"

"That he's still alive?" Patroclus says.

I nod.

"Somehow, he always heals," Patroclus says with a sigh. "Yet I'm never able to contain my fears."

"He's blessed," Dysendra says more to herself than any of us.

"No!" Patroclus shakes his head passionately. "The bastard children of gods are far more cursed than blessed. I stitch him up," Patroclus says as he glances at the battlefield in the distance, "then he charges into the slaughterhouse once again."

I'm feeling slightly sick as I look at the wound, which is the length of a sword, but I force myself to watch every stitch. I know I'll soon have to face far worse sights than this.

"Is it true about his mother?" Wren asks. "Was she really a sea goddess?"

"That," Patroclus replies, "I do not know, and neither does he. The legend says she dipped him in the roaring River Styx three days after his birth to protect him from all wounds. Some say he's immortal. I can only tell you what I've seen with my own eyes. He was unscarred until his sixteenth birthday, his first year of battle in this war."

"So the river doesn't protect him anymore?" I ask.

"I disagree," Patroclus answers. "I've sewn many wounds on many men. A cut like this would kill anyone else. Somehow he always fights again."

"You're Spartan?" I ask, trying to keep the disbelief from my voice. He's wearing Spartan colors, but he's nothing like the other warriors. He's untanned and callous-free, almost delicate.

Patroclus' eyes never leave the flesh he's sewing.

"I was unfit for battle so they trained me as a surgeon. I met Achilles when I was seven and he was nine. Even then, there was little that the best of his mentors could teach him. At sixteen he was forced into this war. As was I – the *son of a king*." His final words are filled with bitterness.

Wren is as shocked as I am. "You're a prince?!"

Patroclus nods. 'Achilles and I never knew our mothers. We're both the illegitimate sons of men who never loved us. At least," he says with a shrug, "his father never disowned him. I was cast from the kingdom, told never to utter my family's name again."

"But *why?*" Wren asks.

"Some called it murder. It wasn't."

Patroclus dips his hand in Briseis' honey-colored ointment, then coats the wound and continues sewing.

"I remember distinctly that Medon and I were both laughing. I was barely seven. He was, I think, the same age. I can't tell you who the visiting king was or where he was from, but I liked Medon, his son, a lot."

Wren and I exchange glances. Patroclus' path to Troy is perhaps even stranger than our own.

"We were near the palace in a wooded area, both of us competing to find the finest fallen tree branches, then calling them swords and daggers. In my head, I can still see us running toward a perfect branch. We grabbed for it at the same time."

"Mine, mine, mine! he said. He was giggling."

Patroclus stares into the distance, then continues.

"No, I touched it first! I yelled. There are nights when that lie still haunts me. He pulled. I pushed. And as he fell, his head hit a rock. I was still laughing: *Come on, get up.* But he didn't."

Patroclus sighs, then tugs on the cut pieces of flesh to pull them together.

"My father was angrier than I'd ever seen him. A staggeringly large amount of gold was given to the visiting king to compensate him for the loss of the crown prince. Then my father sent a courier to Peleus, Achilles' father. An arrangement was made. Father's final words to me were, *Forget my name. You are no longer my son.*"

Patroclus pauses for a moment to shake off the painful memories.

"Achilles and I became loyal friends. I have a life because he *gave* me a life. If I ever have the chance to die so that he will live, I'll do it."

"Did King Peleus treat you like a prince?" I ask.

A hint of a smile forms on Patroclus' lips. "He ignored his son and I equally. For almost two years, our lives were carefree. We spent hours skipping stones, playing our flutes, plucking lyres. Achilles has so many gifts. If allowed to be a musician, he'd be a great one. But his father believed the prophecy: *A son of Peleus shall become the greatest warrior the world will ever know.*"

"I heard he was taught by Chiron the centaur," Wren says, "who once trained Hercules."

Patroclus shakes his head as he tries to hide his amusement.

"No, King Peleus sent us to Sparta. The boys there are taken from their mothers when they're barely waist-high. And those are the last tears they're allowed to cry. The weak and the sick aren't nursed back to health. I survived only because Achilles was my friend, my protector. The generals there matched him against the finest young warriors in the country. It was rare that they even made him stumble. At thirteen, he humiliated the best fighters that his instructors could find to compete against him. To this day, whenever I see sword fighting, it looks like two men hacking at each other with iron sticks. Only Achilles turns it into artistry. Someday you'll see," he smiles, "but hopefully not soon."

"Ody said we could help in the stables," I say.

"Good. I hope I'll never have to stitch either of you back together."

As Wren and I leave the tent, I can't get Briseis' final words out of my head: *Scarp and Ukiah.*

One of those names I'll never forget, Scarp the Defiler. Because of him, my mother is probably dead. Given the chance, I'd kill him myself.

And I'm grateful for Achilles' promise: *They'll both die screaming.*

CHAPTER 5: "There are advantages to being blind."

NARRATOR: JEM

As the sun sets, the wind from the sea is shifting toward the shore, chilling us. As Wren and I huddle together near a campfire, we're grateful that the stew is hot and filling.

"All of these tents, it's like a city," she says softly. "There are thousands and thousands of soldiers here."

"But I haven't seen any dogs."

"Or heard any barking. It's weird."

"You're eating one," says a white-haired man. He's wearing a simple tunic and a wool cloak. "As soon as a mutt so much as yips, he's in the stew pot." He smiles.

Both Wren and I are startled. "Sorry, I ... I ...."

"You didn't notice me?"

"No," I admit.

"There are advantages to being blind and old. People also assume I can't hear. Simply by sitting still, I learn much I should not know. I am Homer, a poet who loves to tell stories. And you?"

"Jem," I say.

"I'm Wren. We're twins."

He turns his head, then twists his neck to an angle that surely must hurt. "And a fine pair you are." He smiles. "Yes, I can still see a little from the side, but only bits and pieces. However, I'm grateful for what remains of my sight."

He points at the milky white lenses of his eyes and adds, "Cataracts, one of the many afflictions of age. My ears tell me that you're not from Athens. Lemnos perhaps?"

I nod, then realize he's still waiting for an answer. "Yes, Lemnos."

"An island that owes allegiance to neither the Grecians nor the Trojans. Both of you, I suspect, know several dialects."

Wren shrugs. "Lots of traders visited our island every week. We had to be able to talk to all of them."

"You can pass for either Greek or Trojan, can't you?" Homer asks.

"Maybe," I answer.

"You're modest. And far wiser than your size would suggest." Homer smiles. "What did you barter on your island?"

"Horses," I say. "My father owned a stable."

"You and your horses have already made the best of all possible friends."

Wren smiles. "Achilles."

"And Odysseus," I add.

Homer nods. "Being at their side places you in a predicament that a storyteller like me often wishes he shared."

Puzzled, we say nothing.

"Under their protection," Homer explains, "you'll probably survive this war, and you'll witness feats of strength and bravery that will seem impossible. But you'll also see much blood, much suffering." He sighs. "Sorry, I'm being far too grim. I always loved Lemnos. Especially your figs. Lord, what I wouldn't give for some fig pudding!"

"Me too," I say, but my voice cracks.

Homer reads my mind. "Your mother made it, didn't she?"

The answer is easy, but I'm trying to keep my emotions from overwhelming me.

"She's dead?" Homer asks softly.

"Yes," I admit for the first time. "Scarp."

"On the day when Achilles awakens, I promise you, that evil man will be dead before the next dawn."

"Good." I almost spit out the word.

"Scarp the Defiler is a man in love with cruelty," Homer says. "He lives for those moments when eyes full of light and life turn to darkness and dullness. It tells me much that Agamemnon regards him highly. You've heard of the Damnati?"

"No," I say.

"They're the eternally damned, the worst of the worst," Homer explains. "Once they were held in Xanthium Prison – rapists, murderers, child molesters – every form of human scum imaginable. And Scarp was their leader."

"He escaped?" Wren asks.

Homer shakes his head. "No. King Agamemnon was so desperate for new soldiers that he emptied Xanthium. And in return Scarp and his followers do things that men of honor like Achilles and Odysseus would refuse."

"Like raiding Lemnos," Wren says.

I poke a stick – *hard* – into the sandy soil in front of me. "I'd like to kill him."

Wren's eyes widen, then she looks away. The words were out of my mouth before I could stop them.

Homer continues. "Agamemnon's army is desperate for horses, goats, chickens, wood – everything. So he's ordered Scarp to strip every island clean, even when all the citizens are Greeks."

"Everything?" Wren asks.

Homer nods. "Stupid, isn't it?! Now that every farmer is a soldier or a slave, who'll plant the crops?"

"Maybe," I say, "Agamemnon thinks the war is almost over."

Homer shrugs. 'Perhaps our king of kings has forgotten that Troy has never been taken since the walls were built a hundred years ago."

I'm stunned. I've just realized that this is a war without honor, a battle without end. And Wren and I are trapped in the middle of it.

"Would it help to talk about how your mother died?" Homer asks.

"Maybe." *I relive that horrible day every night.*

"Then tell me everything," Homer says, "every detail."

"She made us practice what we'd do in case the raiders came," I say. "We thought we were ready."

Wren nods. "They'd attacked a village near the coast a month before."

Homer leans forward. "Tell me as if it's happening now."

CHAPTER 6: "Tell me everything, every detail."

NARRATOR: JEM

Five days earlier, Lemnos.

"Whoa, Beauty. Easy, Brazen." Our four best horses, hitched two by two, slow to a halt. Ten riders seem to be waiting at the crossroads ahead of us.

"Do you recognize any of them?" I ask Wren nervously.

She shades her eyes and squints. "Nobody from Lemnos. And they're definitely not traders."

I nod. "Look at their horses."

"Either those mares are sick or they haven't been feeding them."

Brazen, Black, Beauty, and Bold are our four best runners. Judging by the nags these men are riding, they need horses more than anything else.

They can't have ours. Never.

"If we cut loose the goats, we might be able to outrun them," I say, then glance at the rope that's pulling five angoras and four shorthairs behind our wagon.

"Stick with the plan!" Wren says.

She's right. Part of me would really hate to lose this hay wagon. Dad and I built it so that it would last as long as I lived.

As I'm turning, I see more trouble out of the corner of my eye. "Five more – the grove behind us."

"And another seven," Wren says, "on the ridge."

"Okay, you know what to do."

Wren nods.

I stand on the riding board and make a big show of turning in a circle, pretending that I'm just figuring out what we already know: we're surrounded and seriously outnumbered. While their eyes are on me, Wren is crouched down, carrying out the plan we hoped we'd never have to use.

Two cloth bags have been tucked at our feet, untouched for over a month. One of them is now over her shoulder. Wren's barely visible as she uncouples the two iron pegs that connect the harnesses to the wagon. Seconds later, she has crawled onto Beauty's back.

"I'm ready," she says softly. "Hurry, some of them have started trotting."

Besides the goats, we're about to abandon several bags of buckwheat and oats, eight chickens, a basketful of eggs, and five pots of olive oil – everything we were planning on selling at the village marketplace.

Maybe they'll settle for everything we're leaving in the wagon.

As I grab the cloth bag from underneath the buckboard seat, I glance at the seven riders galloping toward us. No Greek or Trojan colors, no pennants. These guys clearly don't play by the rules. Calling them pirates would be a compliment.

Everyone in Lemnos has heard about the slave labor camps on the shores of Troy. And that's where we're heading unless Wren and I make all the right moves.

Three of the men galloping toward us have spears. One has a heavy net he hopes to trap us in. Two others are swinging bolos over their heads. If those weighted balls wrap around my arms, I won't be able to move.

Wren takes the left team, Beauty and Black, and I take the right, Brazen and Bold.

She slaps the reins against their backsides and her team surges forward. Somehow they seem to know that this situation is life-or-death serious.

I grab my own twin bridles and follow, only a few moments behind.

Two of the men are on foot. Each is carrying a long pike, which is usually seen on the decks of large ships. One of the men has a nose that looks as if it's been broken countless times during brawls. The other seems to have no right hand.

I look closer: somehow he's attached an animal claw where his fingers would normally be. On his forearm is a tattoo identical to the other man's: an octopus, each tentacle grasping and choking everything within its reach.

Both men are now standing in the middle of the road with their sharp poles crossed, daring us to break through.

They're bluffing. They've got to be!

These men are desperate for healthy animals, and surely they realize that their sharp poles will cripple our horses.

"Trust me, Bold. Trust me, Brazen," I say.

Since my horses aren't wearing blinders, they can see the deadly pikes just as well as I can. They continue galloping.

"Use your bag!" I yell to Wren, but once again I've under-estimated her.

Wren's charging straight at the ragged thief with the misshapen nose. She's gripping the bag in her right hand as if it's a ball. She aims, releases, and ...

Pow!

Connects!

Pepper explodes over the brute's chest and face. Blinded, he drops the pole and tries to brush away the thousand black bits that cover his eyes.

The endless hours my father spent teaching Wren how to hit a target have paid off many times. Anyone stupid enough to yell *I'll bet you throw like a girl* always regrets it.

I twirl my bag by its handle once, twice, then launch it. The claw-man ducks, then tosses his pike aside.

His crazy eyes tell me that he's not afraid. I'm in trouble.

His claw hand is slashing at my leg as I gallop past.

Rip!

The sharp talons are digging into my leg, pulling hard at my pants. I'm being pulled to the ground!

The fabric rips, then gives way. I sit upright and charge forward.

My sister points. Seven more riders have joined the chase. Wren and I separate, abandoning the dirt path. Our attackers are whipping their horses, pushing them to their limits.

I never ask our lead horse to give me everything he's got unless I'm in desperate trouble. It's time to say the magic words;

"Fly, Brazen, fly!"

I hang on as we surge forward. He's a horse who would run himself to the edge of death if we asked him to.

Bold is wild-eyed, but he knows we're in trouble. He'll keep up for as long as he can.

No one knows these woods better than Wren and I do. I stay off the trails until I'm certain that I'm not being followed, then slow the pace.

Home is two hours away, and even though there's no longer any danger, I'm nervous. Perhaps I'm imagining things.

Every so often, I think I see movement atop ridges. Trappers are rare in this area, but Mom barters with all of them when we need to. None of them are close friends, but more importantly, none of them are enemies.

When I finally reach home, I'm relieved to see Wren. She and Mom are in their muck-raking clothes and they've finished grooming Black and Beauty.

Mom rushes toward me. "I was worried."

"We had to leave the wagon behind."

She holds me closely and whispers, "You and Wren are what's important, nothing else."

I see a plate of food atop a fence post and ask, "For me?"

She nods, then finally releases me. Her heart is beating as fast as mine is.

After washing my hands, I devour the bread, olives, and apple she set aside for me.

"Do we have to clean the stables now?" I whine.

"It has to be done," Mom says, "and hard work will help us forget about this morning." She points at a pair of scissors and says, "Later, I'll trim your hair." She smiles as she adds what I've heard her say so many times before. "I can't have you looking like someone's unloved brat."

Reluctantly, I change into my muck-raking clothes. They used to belong to Dad.

"Hurry up," Wren says. "Brazen's all worked up about something and I need your help."

"Thanks," says a voice next to the stable entrance.

Mom drops the grooming brush she's holding and grabs a garden hoe off the wall.

Someone calmly enters.

"You led us right to your horses. We had lookouts on every ridge just in case you slipped away from us."

Five more men now block the entrance. My eyes are frantically searching for something I can sneak into my pockets, something I can use to hurt these men who've been plundering Lemnos for weeks.

The scissors are too far away. Grooming brushes? No, not heavy enough.

Bridles? Too large.

A loose bit. Yes. And a broken stirrup – even better. I edge my way toward them.

"I see yah, boy. And I'll break that hand if it moves again." He pulls a knife from his belt and tells me, "Don't make me spill your guts right in front of your pretty mama." He smiles.

"Scarp, there are twenty horses," one of the newcomers says to the man who just threatened to slice my belly open.

"I can count," snarls Scarp. He's a brute of a man with greasy black hair and brown stumps for teeth. "I want every one of the horses on the ships before sundown. These four," he points at Brazen, Bold, Beauty, and Black, "will haul the wagon."

Scarp grabs the hoe from my mother, then slaps her. *Hard.*

I hate this man more than I've ever hated anyone.

"Tie these two in the wagon, gag 'em," he says. "I'll handle the woman."

One of the men laughs. A heartbeat later, Scarp's knife is buried in the wooden post next to his head.

"Out, all of you!" Scarp orders.

* * *

Leather straps are cutting into my hands and ankles. The harder I try to break them or pull them off, the more I bleed. The broken-nosed man used reins and bridles to tie me to the side boards of our wagon. Then he loaded two heavy sacks of oats onto Wren, who's also bound and gagged.

Our wagon is overflowing with everything of value that my mother and father spent a lifetime acquiring.

"Where's the woman?"

"Tied in the stables."

"She'll fetch a fine price."

"Not anymore."

"Scarp?"

The other man nods.

The broken-nosed man fingers the blade of an ax that's roped to the back of the buckboard, then changes the subject. "The Greeks need wood for funeral pyres and campfires. They're paying five silvers per tree. Five silvers!"

"But it takes a slave to chop it down and a strong horse to drag it," another man says. "They want pigs, wild boars too – easy money."

One of the men laughs. "Have yah ever tried to catch a wild boar? They're mean. And good runners."

A man with a torch grins. "The boss has a plan: burn the trees, make 'em run right into yer nets."

"What if you burn down the island?" one of the men asks.

"As long as I get my silver, I don't give a damn."

Scarp slams the stable doors, then hurries toward the wagon. The men immediately become silent.

"Give us a good start," Scarp says to the man with the torch, "then flush the pigs toward the boats."

I'm filled with fear and dread that he's thinking more about hogs than my mother. Why isn't she in the wagon with us?!

I'm biting into my gag, angry with these stupid, stupid men who've never farmed and never raised horses or herded cattle. All they know how to do is destroy things, not build them.

They're willing to set fire to half of Lemnos to get a hundred wild boars. After all of the farmers are dead and their fields burned, the Greeks will have no flour for bread, no logs for their funeral pyres.

"Who went ahead with the stallions?" the broken-nosed man asks.

"Ukiah."

"Damn it!" Scarp says. "Last time he clawed half of them."

I cringe at the thought.

Scarp grabs the reins, then flays the backs of our horses with his lash. They lurch forward even though they're pulling far too heavy a load.

The man with the torch hurries toward the cypress grove behind the stable as our wagon leaves.

I strain against the leather straps that bind my feet and hands. I'm desperately trying to look all around me. *Where?! Where is she?!*

The gag in my mouth is so tight that it's hurting me, but even so, I try to shout one last word.

"Mom?!"

There's no response.

Too late to duck, I see a man swinging a shovel at my head.

* * *

When I finally come to, my head is throbbing and I can't see straight.

Wren and I are on the top level of some kind of ship. It's night and cold winds from the Aegean are blowing toward the shore.

A huge man holding a knife approaches us. "You fight me, I'll cut yah. Understand?!"

I nod.

He removes my gag, then slices through the ties around my wrists and ankles. He does the same for Wren.

"Everyone rows. No excuses," he says as he leaves.

I'm too dizzy to stand but I manage to make my way to the side of the boat, then puke over the edge.

"Are you okay?" Wren whispers.

Nothing is okay, *nothing*. "Have you seen Mom?"

"No."

On shore, two men are arguing.

"It won't fit, I tell yah!" one of them shouts.

"Then we'll *make* it fit."

On shore I hear the splintering of wood, then groan as I realize what "it" is.

Our wagon. What took three weeks to build is being kicked to pieces in seconds. Soon only the wheels are recognizable. The splintered wood they've tossed onto the deck is now worthless for anything but firewood.

Someone hits a drumhead and shouts, *"Pull!* Put your backs into it."

The light of a half moon shows me that there are three triremes lining the shore. I glance at the deck of the ship we're on and see nothing but oars and rowing positions. That's when I realize we're on the same narrow type of craft. Triremes are built for speed. There are three tiers of oars; a full crew is two hundred rowers. But even though there are no more than forty of us rowing, we're moving.

In the deeper water of the bay, we can see a two-mast ship. Our thin boat is being used to ferry people and cargo onto it.

Wren and I are near the back of the boat. Behind us is an orange and black pottery urn that could hold at least fifty pitchers of water. But it's nearly full of a chalk-colored paste and the fumes from it are making me sick to my stomach.

One of the crew, a guy no more than fourteen, sees that Wren is curious. "Don't touch it," he warns.

"Why?" she asks.

"'Cuz it stings – white phosphorus. We coat arrow tips with it, set 'em afire, then land a few shafts on another boat. Once it starts burning, it's like the sun coming out at midnight." He glances back at Lemnos. "Kinda like yer island right now."

Huge fires are raging for as far as I can see. And I accept the truth:

Mom burned to death in the stables.

I look away and try not to think about it.

CHAPTER 7: "He'll be dead before dawn."

NARRATOR: JEM

Ody has given us jobs at the stables and we're grateful for them. We groom the horses, feed them, put ointment on their wounds, and hitch them to chariots. It feels good to be useful.

I drifted off to sleep last night with Homer's words about Scarp in my head:

On the day when Achilles awakens, I promise you, that evil man will be dead before the next dawn.

I've *got* to be there, *got* to make sure that Scarp the Defiler and Ukiah the Claw pay for what they've done.

Long before sunrise, I quietly pull on leggings, a tunic, and a heavy cloak, then sneak from our tent toward the stables. The horses seem to be as restless as I am.

Inside, I'm shocked to see the man who only a day earlier seemed close to death.

"If you're going to Scarp's camp, I want to help."

Bridle in hand, Achilles turns but says nothing.

"He killed my mother."

His jaw hardens. "I cannot let you fight the Damnati."

"I could drive your chariot. Our horses are the best you've got.'

Achilles hesitates as he considers what I've said. Then his mouth begins to form the word I don't want to hear.

"Brazen and Bold will listen to *me*, not you!" I blurt out the words, saying them with far more emotion than I should.

But he hasn't said *no*. Not yet. I watch in agony as his massive chest breathes in, then out.

"You'd promise to stay with the chariot?"

I nod.

"And follow my orders?"

"Yes, sir."

He nods. *I'm going!*

"I'll hitch the horses two-by-two in front of your chariot."

"Which of the four is fastest?" Achilles asks.

"Brazen."

"Then he's in the lead; the others will follow. All will need chainmail for armor; Scarp will have archers."

"When will we leave?" I ask.

"After I get us some bread and dried fish. We'll arrive at the new Damnati camp near sunrise. Our spies say that they haven't finished building their watchtowers yet."

"How many soldiers are coming?" I ask.

"My men will be here soon."

"Good," I say, even though he's ignored my question.

* * *

Two guys are shuffling toward the stables. One's really short. The other guy can't stop yawning. His hair looks as if he hasn't washed it in weeks.

"Are you Jem?" the short guy asks.

I nod.

"Achilles said you could pick the best horses for us."

"Okay, sure," I say.

"I'm Three Toe."

I glance at his left foot: three toes.

"And everyone calls me Two Blade," says the guy with bad hair. He lifts a huge battle ax, points to the first blade, twists it, then runs his thumb over the second edge. He spends a *lot* more time sharpening that ax than he spends thinking about his hair.

"Where's your armor?" I ask.

"Metal makes noise," Three Toe tells me.

Two Blade grins. "We're gunna surprise 'em."

"Achilles likes to have a light crew," Two Blade adds.

Three Toe has two leather bags at his feet. I reach for one and say, "Let me help you."

I badly misjudge the heaviness of the bag, then stumble.

"Sorry," Three Toe says, "shoulda warned you."

Two Blade grins and points at his friend. "Slingers – they always bring their own rocks."

I pick up the five grey balls that I spilled and state the obvious. "Lead."

"Lead's best – one rock will do it," Three Toe says. "Iron's not nearly as good – you've gotta two-ball 'em to drop 'em, yah know?"

The look on my face tells him that I have no idea what he's talking about.

Three Toe unties a simple leather slingshot from his belt, then offers it to me so that I can look it over. It's the kind where you release one of the two strings and then let the rock fly.

He loads his slingshot and says, "Knot hole, center post."

Bonk!

As the lead ball bounces off the knot hole, Two Blade catches it on the rebound and points at his friend. "He's amazing. Hits anything he wants to."

I was expecting a lot more men to be going with us. But perhaps Achilles' plan is to slit Scarp's filthy throat while he's sleeping, then leave.

I saddle Vesuvius, a strong Arabian, for Two Blade. Three Toe gets Dappled, a spotted mare who's easier to handle.

I push seven spears into the chariot's side holders, then slip on a hardened-leather chest plate, cowhide arm shields, and lambskin leg protectors.

Achilles arrives with bread and dried fish, then hands some to each of us. He pulls a leather strap over his chest and positions a shield onto his back.

"Scarp will die," he says quietly to me. "You have my word." Then he steps into the chariot by my side.

I flick the reins. Brazen, Bold, Beauty, and Black are eager to begin this new adventure, and they quickly pull us onto the chariot path.

* * *

For the next hour, we endure a hard, cold rain, which just might give us an advantage. Scarp's camp is the highest point in the area, but his watchmen won't be able to hear us coming.

The pathway we're following is next to a river, which is overflowing because of the downpour. The route we're taking is almost all uphill.

Occasionally we pass soothsayers and holy men who have been out all night praying beside the river.

"Blood has desecrated Poseidon's holy waters!" shouts one of them as we pass. "Corpses have defiled the Xanthos. Beware the sea god's wrath!"

"The River Xanthos has become the River of Death!" says another.

The heavy rain finally decreases but howling winds continue. The gusts are whipping the waves to waist-high levels.

The first rays of the new day show us that Scarp's campsite is very new, no more than a day old. No fencing has been built for their horses or pigs. The campsite is far larger than I expected it to be; at least two hundred tents are scattered atop the hillside.

But what shocks me most is the number of corpses next to the river, none of them soldiers, all defenseless. Dozens of the bodies are children; many of them seem to have been helping their mothers wash clothes.

"This was a fishing village," Achilles says to me. Anger is rising in his voice.

And now it's the home of the Damnati: the worst of the worst, the irredeemable, the eternally damned.

Achilles' body tenses. He seizes a spear, then pivots toward the top of a ridge. A guard has spotted us and I watch in horror as he raises a battle horn to his lips. He's too far away for any of our weapons to reach.

Yet Achilles takes aim, then launches the bronze-tipped blade.

As the horn touches the guard's mouth, Achilles' spear pierces his throat. His body crumples to the ground. The only sounds we hear are the roaring of the river and the howling of the wind.

Achilles has done the impossible. We're still undetected.

He points at a man crawling from one of the tents near the top of the hill. "That, I suspect, is the night guard's replacement. We must move quickly."

Achilles points at a bend in the river and says to Three Toe and Two Blade, "I will need your help there soon. Jem, go with them, tie our chariot to the trees."

"I'd feel safer with you," I mumble.

"As you wish." Achilles shifts his shield to his right arm, then says, "Climb onto my back."

My eyes must show my amazement because he quickly adds, "We won't be fast enough with you on foot."

I do as I'm told.

With astonishing speed, we reach the top of a cliff. The river is churning below. Achilles scans the area, which is covered with nets both large and small. This is apparently where many of the fishermen's wives repaired nets, an area where they could clearly see the Aegean Sea as well as their husbands' returning ships.

My eyes widen with dread as I see the new guard running toward the downed night watchman. In seconds, he'll sound the battle horn.

"Achilles!" I point.

"There's no need to waste a spear on him. Everything we need is at our feet."

The alert sounds. And I'll confess that I'm beginning to panic.

Achilles pounds on his shield with the hilt of his sword and bellows, "We've come to kill you! *All* of you!"

Anyone not awakened by the guard's horn has now been jolted into alertness by Achilles' booming voice. Men are pouring from the tents, throwing on armor as they emerge.

Their chest plates are ordinary but their helmets are like nothing I've ever seen. The front visor has been sculpted to look like an enraged face, an image of one of the Furies.

The Furies are demons from the Underworld sent to drive men mad. There's no escape from them.

"How will we know which one's Scarp?" I ask.

My question goes unanswered. The army of demons is racing toward us.

Behind us is a cliff. The raging Xanthos River is two hundred feet below. There's not even the slightest chance of escape.

"Jem, get behind me!"

I'm trembling, terrified by what I see. The Furies themselves will soon tear me apart.

"Don't move!" Achilles tells me.

The Damnati are screaming, enraged that intruders have found their hilltop hideaway. Half of the men running toward us are now less than a spear's-throw away.

Achilles widens his stance and grabs the largest of the fishing nets spread out around us. Only the biggest fishing trawlers on the Aegean can handle such nets, which entrap a thousand fish.

Achilles tugs *hard* on the net, gathers more of it into his arms, then pulls again. And again.

Scores of men fall as the webbing entangles them. Achilles throws an end of the net over their heads, then rushes to gather up all of the edges. Each time he yanks on the mesh, more of the Damnati stumble and fall. At least a hundred men are now entrapped in his web.

"Jem," Achilles shouts, "do you trust me?"

"Yes." I have no other choice.

"Then climb onto my back. And do ... not ... let ... go!"

I tighten my arms around his neck and lock my hands together. My life depends on it.

I cringe as he begins dragging his *catch* to the edge of the cliff.

More and more of Scarp's warriors join the tug of war. A hundred men are pulling on the edges of the net, attempting to save their fellow soldiers from being thrown to their deaths. If the rocks don't kill them, the raging waters will.

"Take a deep breath!" Achilles says.

And to my horror, he jumps.

We fall. Until we don't.

I open my eyes and see that Achilles and I, as well as our captured attackers, are dangling from the edge of the cliff, all of us suspended between Heaven and Hell.

The corners of the netting are still caught inside the vice grip of his hands and arms.

Above us we hear, "Pull! Pull!"

A hint of a smile forms on Achilles' lips.

"Fools."

He pumps his legs as if we're sitting on a child's wooden swing. We sway in the breeze. And he pulls again.

Each second, a dozen more men fall from the cliff into the webbing and we move nearer to the rapids.

Finally the weight below the cliff edge exceeds the weight above. And things begin happening scary-fast. Two hundred of Scarp's scum are now falling with us.

Achilles releases his hold on the rope-like netting. Suddenly nothing but raining men surround us.

Splurshhhhh!

We hit the water and descend one spear length, two, then three, and four. I'm desperate for another breath of air. The churning water is blood red. That's when I remember the soothsayer's words.

The river god is angry. The River Xanthos has become the River of Death!

As we hit the rocky bottom of the river, I almost lose my grip around Achilles' neck. He bends his legs at the knees, then thrusts us upward.

We arrive in the middle of the many men he pulled off the cliff.

As I gulp in air, I see a whirlpool capture a man, twist him into an impossible shape, then drown him. All of our attackers are now battling the river as well as us.

The current is carrying us downstream. As we approach a huge boulder, Achilles seizes a floating fishing net with both hands and hooks one end onto the many branches of a tree on the river bank.

The thick webbing holds.

My eyes widen with fear as we rush toward a cluster of boulders. Achilles repositions his legs to cushion the blow, then loops some of the mesh around the rocks.

For the moment, we're being held in the middle of these raging waters by the net. We're slightly downstream from the whirlpool. It's seven-foot eye seems to see each of our attackers, then dashes them against the rocks.

If the river god was looking for the perfect moment to avenge himself against the Damnati who defiled it with innocent children, he has found it.

As lifeless bodies float past us, Achilles heaves them onto the net. Corpse by corpse, our bridge grows. Until finally we are able to walk over the faces of the thugs who were certain only minutes ago that they would hack us into pieces, then feed us to their pigs.

As we step onto the river bank, I hear the rumble of horses. The Furies have found us once again. At least fifty of them await us.

Their swords are drawn. They have no intention of allowing us to walk from this valley.

Achilles sees the fear in my eyes and reassures me.

"Hell has no limits, Jem. The dead can never fill it."

But I'm unnerved by the feeling that their leader is staring at me. He lifts the visor on his helmet and smiles broadly, showing me the hideous brown stumps he calls teeth.

Scarp.

"Bring me the boy!" he shouts. And his men begin their charge.

Achilles points at our chariot near a grove of trees.

"Hide there, then do not move!"

As I dash for shelter, I grab one of the Damnati shields that's littering the banks of the river.

I crouch at the bottom of the chariot and try to make my body into as small a target as possible. Part of me wants to close my eyes, but, as always, I cannot. I stare in amazement.

Achilles, shield-less and sword-less, is sprinting at thirty of the Damnati, all on horseback. His war cry is ear-splitting. They must believe he's insane.

Achilles leaps atop a boulder, springs toward a tree, then launches himself from its trunk. Panther-like, his eyes are locked onto one man, Scarp the Defiler, and one goal, his swift death.

Moments ago, Achilles was below the Damnati. Now he's forced them to reverse their horses and climb uphill with the sun in their eyes.

Scarp has no idea what's about to happen. He's trying to control his skittish horse. Seconds ago, Achilles was a hundred paces away. Now he's coming at the Damnati leader from the side, out of his line of sight.

Scarp's eyes flare, but it's already too late when he sees Achilles in mid-leap. The two collide; Scarp falls and *pop,* his shoulder dislocates as his body hits the ground.

Cat-like, Achilles lands on his feet.

Scarp's eyes flash open. Death is above him, staring him in the face. And a heartbeat later, his neck is inside the vice-like bend of Achilles' elbow.

The demon who killed my mother is now wide eyed with fear.

Crack!

I jump, startled by the intensity of the sound of breaking vertebrae. Scarp's head is now dangling like a dead chicken's.

The sight leaves me gasping.

Achilles charges into the midst of the riders, grabs their arms or legs and pulls them to the ground. He seizes a sword, then gyrates, twists, and turns. Several of the men are now in pieces.

Their stallions panic, then stampede over the men who rode them into this valley. Their hooves tear what's left of Scarp's lieutenants to bits, grinding them into the mud and grit.

One of the Damnati is screaming out a warning to his fellow survivors, "This is Achilles – *Achilles the god!*" All of them have realized that they are battling no ordinary man.

Twenty of Scarp's cavalry remain. They turn, searching for an escape path. But two men on horseback now block their retreat:

Two Blade and Three Toe!

"Achilles!" shouts Two Blade. He tosses his double-bladed battle ax over the heads of the Damnati and into the hands of his friend.

Achilles grabs an iron ring attached to the ax's handle, digs his left heel into the dirt, and transforms himself into an ever-spinning death machine. A river of Damnati blood begins flowing down the hillside.

Without warning, arrows come raining down. Scarp's archers have found us.

From somewhere above, I hear a cry: "Jem, throw me a spear!"

It's Two Blade! There's fear in his voice.

Thud!

An arrow hits the shield above my head, then bounces off.

Thump!Thump!Thump!

Three shafts slice through the side of our chariot. One of the bronze tips is no more than a hand's length from my face.

I'm cowering at the bottom of the chariot, paralyzed with fear.

Neigh!

The horses are afraid, not understanding that the chainmail armor covering them will stop the arrows.

"Throw ... me ... a ... spear!"

I can hear the desperation in Two Blade's voice. He gave his battle ax to Achilles and now he's armed only with a dagger.

He's relying on me.

There are seven spears inside the two leather-strap holders of this chariot. They're within easy reach.

But Achilles' final words to me were *Hide there, then do not move!*

More archers are now above us, at least ten.

My shield isn't large, barely enough to protect my shoulders and head. As soon as the archers see me carrying spears to Two Blade, I'll become their main target.

To get the weapons into his hands, I'd need to run thirty paces in the open, then toss the shafts far over my head to the ridge where he's standing.

"Help me!" he screams.

Do not move!

I'm trembling, curled into a tight ball on the floor of Achilles' chariot with a shield covering me.

"Bastards!"

It's Three Toe's voice. He's near Two Blade.

Bang!Bang!Bang!

Triple shots of lead balls are hitting the archers' chest plates.

Boink!

Another connects with a bronze helmet. High above me, one of the Damnati is screaming. And his cry is coming nearer and nearer.

THUD!

His body slams to the ground no more than ten paces from me.

CRACK!

Another body lands uncomfortably close to the horses. Most of the man's bones are now broken but he's not dead yet. His death throes overwhelm all other sounds.

Neighhhhh! Neighhhhh!

Brazen, not easily spooked, rears onto his back legs.

As the chariot shakes, I peek my head above the top edge. Brazen is turned enough so that I can see his eyes. They're filled with agony and confusion.

I'm the one who's supposed to protect *him,* help ease his pain. And I've failed completely.

I stick my head out far enough to see an arrow in his chest. As soon as Brazen reared up, his chainmail shifted, giving the archers a clear shot at one of the few areas where he was unprotected.

"AAAAAH!"

Two Blade is screaming. I don't have to see the wound to know that he's been hurt badly.

The downpour of arrows has ended. Achilles is leaping from boulder to boulder to reach the archers. On the ridge above me, I hear hoof beats, then galloping. The archers are fleeing while they can.

I force myself onto my knees and stare at what my cowardice has caused. Two Blade has an arrow shaft in his right arm. Three Toe's face has been clawed.

Because of me, our mission is not finished: Ukiah the Claw still lives.

If I'd delivered the spears, the archers above us would be dead. Two Blade would not be dying. And Brazen would be uninjured.

Overwhelmed with grief and shame, all I can do is tremble.

"More are coming!" Achilles says as he pushes the reins into my hands.

Achilles removes a blanket from the side of the chariot, uses it to wipe away blood from his left thigh, then presses the same blanket against the wound on Brazen's chest.

Snap.

With a quick twist of his wrist, Achilles breaks off an arrow shaft, then pulls it from my brave horse. He neighs in pain but quivers less as Achilles ties the blanket tightly around his wound.

"Can you do it, boy?" Achilles asks Brazen. "Can you help us get home?"

A spear barely misses Three Toe as he mounts his horse. Achilles lowers Two Blade to the floor of our chariot, then positions his legs so that he won't slide out.

"Get us out of here, Jem," Achilles shouts.

I flick the reins against our horses' backs and watch them again do the impossible. Brazen, Black, Beauty, and Bold all possess strength and courage no matter what horrors they're asked to face.

I do not.

CHAPTER 8: A Deep, Deep Sleep

NARRATOR: JEM

I'm shivering in the night air outside the tent where Patroclus sews up wounded soldiers. He's done his best and has gone to bed.

Two Blade will probably die. Brazen too.

I'm watching Orion climb higher in the sky. Wren's nearby, worried about me, not allowing me out of her sight.

Dysendra touches my arm. "Sleep. Their souls will have departed by sunrise."

I'm exhausted, but I can't imagine sleeping. Not now, not after what I've seen and done today.

I thought that watching Scarp die would lessen the pain I feel whenever I think about my mother. Instead, I'm haunted by the sight and sounds of his death.

And I'm tortured by my own failings.

Throw ... me ... a ... spear!

I can't get Two Blade's words out of my head. Because I was a coward, we're going to lose one of our best soldiers.

As each hour passes, he's growing paler. When the light of dawn arrives, he'll be as white as the funeral shroud we'll wrap his body in.

It's true that Two Blade never should have given his only major weapon to Achilles. But *I* should've done something besides cower inside the chariot with a shield over my head.

Brazen is nearby, lying on his side, near death. All because of one arrow, an arrow that never would have been shot if I'd done the one thing that Two Blade begged me to do.

"Ody told me," Wren says, "that all of Scarp's men dip their weapons in horse dung or plague blood, anything that will infect a cut."

Dysendra sighs. "And these wounds are deep."

I cringe. In other words, there's no hope.

As I return to the stench inside the tent, the first thing that catches my eye is the pile of blood-stained clothing we stripped off of Two Blade and Achilles. Next to it is the dark-green blanket that Achilles tied over Brazen's wound.

Before the blanket was pressed against Brazen's chest, he was shaking uncontrollably. Moments later, he was strong enough to help pull our chariot.

How is that possible? I force myself to relive every heartbeat of what happened.

Achilles pulled the blanket from the side of the chariot, then he wiped the blood off his thigh. Finally he tied that tattered old thing around Brazen's wound.

That's when I realize I haven't tried *everything*. Not yet.

The water in the cauldron that Dysendra uses for laundry is almost boiling. I almost burn my fingers as I fill a bowl, then lower myself to the ground next to the bloody blanket.

Wren looks at me with concern in her eyes. "Are you all right?"

I nod, afraid that my voice will shake and betray me.

Before Dysendra throws all of the clothes into the cauldron, I have to try something, something a bit crazy.

Dysendra and Wren watch as I dip the bloody part of the blanket into the hot water. I dip and squeeze, then do it again. And again and again. When there's not even a drop of blood left in the fabric, I throw it into the laundry cauldron.

"I can do that, you know," Dysendra says softly.

"I know."

I dig through the pile of clothes until I find Achilles' tunic, then I squeeze the red from its white folds.

Bowl in hand, I walk oh-so-slowly to Two Blade's side. I place the palm of my hand next to his nostrils. He's barely breathing. I know from sad experience that he'll soon be dead.

I place clean bandages into the red-stained water, then begin rewrapping his horrible wound.

"Jem, don't," Dysendra says. "You'll infect the cut."

"He's going to die anyway," I say bluntly. "You said so yourself."

Dysendra nods.

"And I have to try this."

She bites her lip and looks away.

My bowl of precious red water is now three-quarters empty. I carry it to where Brazen is lying on the cold ground, then bathe his wound with it.

His eyes flicker open. They're full of the darkness of near-death. I soak a clean bandage with the possibly infected liquid, then press it over the hole where the arrow entered.

Patroclus said that Achilles goes into a deep, deep sleep after he's been seriously wounded. I'm hoping that the same thing happens to Two Blade and Brazen.

Finally I curl up next to Brazen and allow myself to relax. When I awaken, this trusting, loyal horse, who patiently allowed me to pull on his mane when I was just a stupid kid, will probably be cold and dead.

Because I cowered, trembled, and did nothing.

CHAPTER 9: A Golden Apple / The Truth

NARRATOR: WREN

I'm not sure why, but all at once the breakfast tent becomes very quiet. Everyone is staring at something in back of Jem. I turn.

Two Blade is towering over him. Jem flinches, afraid that he'll strike him, then call him a coward.

Two Blade laughs.

"Do I really look that bad?! As if I've returned from the dead?!"

"I ... I...," Jem stammers.

"Dysendra says you saved me. I don't remember a thing, but I know I'm here because of you."

Moments later, fifty men surround us, overwhelmed with joy. One of our best warriors is back, soon to be as strong as ever.

After Jem and Three Toe have told and then retold yesterday's amazing adventures, the talk around the campfire becomes more serious. Soon the soldiers are whispering about who they trust –

Achilles and Odysseus – and who they fear – Agamemnon.

"Odysseus is a king who rules with wisdom," Two Blade says, "a man worth dying for."

"A king?!" I say. The expression on Jem's face tells me that he's as astonished as I am.

"Yes, of Ithaca, one of the western islands," Three Toe says.

"Why isn't *he* king of kings?" Jem asks.

Dysendra has just brought us another plate of hogback ham. She answers the question.

"Because Agamemnon rules by fear. Someday he'll kill one too many of his own commanders for not bringing him enough virgins. Until then, the regiments must obey him." Her face hardens. "If I'm ever tired of living, I'll slit his throat myself."

She sees the astonishment in my eyes and explains.

"I was married once. And free. All of Agamemnon's slaves are women. After he conquers a city, he kills every male, even the babies. Then he burns the crops and all of the homes. The women and girls who please him become his whores. The day I was captured was the only day of my life that I was glad to be ugly."

Dysendra lifts the heavy meat platter and hurries to the next table.

"No one seems to want this war," I say softly.

"Or think that Agamemnon should be the king of kings," Jem adds. "How could that happen?"

"Would you like to hear the myth or the truth?"

Startled, I almost tip over my plate. Homer, like a soft-footed cat, has somehow crept within inches of us without making a sound.

"Sit with us, Homer," Three Toe says with a smile. "Tell us your tales."

He shakes his head. "Not until you answer my question. Would you like to hear the myth or the truth?"

"Both!" I say.

Homer laughs. "You flatter me. Which first?"

"The myth," Jem says.

"As you wish." Homer tilts his head toward the heavens as if the Muses are whispering in his ears. "It all began with an apple."

"An apple?!" I say.

Homer nods. "A *golden* apple to be exact. Years before this war, when Prince Paris of the House of Priam was but a lump in Queen Hecuba's belly, she dreamed that her son would one day cause the fall of Troy. So soon after his birth, she abandoned the baby on the slopes of Mount Ida. Shepherds raised him as one of their own, unaware of his royal blood. As he grew to manhood, young Paris tended to the flocks faithfully. One fateful day he became an accidental guest at the wedding of King Peleus and the sea goddess Thetis. It was a celebration so grand that it was attended by the gods themselves."

"Even Zeus?" Three Toe asks.

Homer smiles. "Even the lord of lightning. But Paris was not the only unexpected guest. The Goddess of Strife soon arrived – quite uninvited – and rolled a golden apple onto a path just as three of the most breathtaking of Mount Olympus' fair ladies were strolling by: tempestuous Hera, wise Athena, and the exquisite Aphrodite. Inscribed on the apple were the words ...

TO THE MOST BEAUTIFUL

"And each of the goddesses claimed that *she* was the most deserving of such a rare prize."

Jem and I lean closer, not wanting to miss a word.

"To settle the dispute, Zeus assigned Paris the task of selecting a winner. The young shepherd gazed upon their splendor, listened to their enchanting voices, and inhaled their intoxicating scents."

Homer's eyebrows dance with delight as he adds, "All three goddesses offered him bribes."

Three Toe is grinning like a kid.

"Hera promised Paris that he could one day rule over a vast empire. Athena

tempted him with glory, saying she'd
make him a hero during a war that would
reshape the map for all time. And then
Aphrodite offered him the most beautiful
woman in the world."

I glance at Jem. His eyes are wide with
wonder.

"But the goddess neglected to mention
that the ravishing beauty, Helen, was
already married ...," Homer pauses, "...
to a jealous man whose brother, King
Agamemnon, was a ruler who loved gold
gained during battle above all other
things."

My eyes widen. This myth contains a lot
of truth.

"And Paris, the young fool, accepted
Aphrodite's offer. Then the goddess
revealed to him that he was the son of
King Priam and told him to insist on his
birthright. But the true winner on that
day was not Aphrodite, not Paris, and
certainly not Helen, but Strife herself.
For Strife loves wars, especially long
ones."

Homer inhales deeply, then continues.
"And what of the woman now known as Helen
of Troy? She possesses - in *abundance* -

a beauty that makes all men gasp. But no love. No loyalty. And definitely no devotion."

Homer bends lower, cocks his head to the side, and locates a puddle containing a seemingly bottomless supply of mud. He covers his hands with it, then continues.

"And that is why we are now mired in mud, stuck in the middle of this endless war." He smiles as he raises his hands, both dripping. "Strife ruled on that day, and she still reigns supreme."

The men raise their tin cups in his honor. "To Homer!"

A ram's horn sounds the call to assembly and all of the warriors rush toward their chariots.

"Did you enjoy my tale?" Homer asks.

"Very much," I say. "How much was true?"

He winks. "Believe what you like. It's more fun that way."

* * *

The Truth

WREN

The busiest part of our day is always just after sunset when the battles end. Chariot after chariot arrives at our stables. The men, exhausted, are often moving slowly. Most are glazed with sweat, splattered with mud and blood. Those who are seriously wounded have already been taken to Patroclus' tent to die or to be stitched together so they can fight another day.

We clean the chariots, groom and feed the horses, then hurry toward the cooks' campfires. Usually most of the soldiers have already eaten and departed.

Tonight as we walk toward the cooking cauldrons, we're pleased to see that Ody and Homer haven't finished dinner.

One of Agamemnon's imperial guards arrives silently and scans the area. Ody rises quickly, then rushes to find out what the man wants.

The guard removes his helmet, a sign of respect.

"Sir, our king of kings has sent me for the blind man."

Ody frowns. "And may I ask why?"

"To kill him. Our king has heard rumors that the old man dares to mock him."

"Please assure Lord Agamemnon that such gossip is false."

"Sir," the guard says softly, "he's old and worthless."

"In some eyes, not mine," Ody tells him.

"Why do you defend him?"

Ody arches an eyebrow. "Because he tells a fine tale."

The guard shifts uncomfortably. "I was ordered to return with a head."

Ody hesitates, then smiles. "The man Agamemnon is seeking died in the plague tent just hours ago. And neither of us would want to risk our beloved leader's health by delivering a plague-infested skull."

The guard sighs with relief. "Once again, sir, I'm in your debt."

"And I am in yours," Ody says. "Beheadings always ruin my dinner."

As soon as Agamemnon's executioner is out of hearing range, Ody roars, "Homer, tell us a tale! And tonight let's hear the *truth* of how we came to rot here on the shores of Troy."

"The truth?!" Homer says with a grin. "That you shall hear if you'll set me down next to a warm fire and hand me another bowl of what our cook calls stew."

So Jem and I guide our white-haired friend to a tree stump next to a campfire. Soldiers gather round, eager for another story.

"Four long years ago, a shallow man with shining hair," Homer begins, "named Prince Paris set sail from King Priam's palace in Troy. His destination? Lord Agamemnon's court in Greece. His mission? To sign a simple trade agreement. But a flirtatious beauty named Helen caught his eye. How, history will ask, did one foolish man and one lustful woman start a war that has killed thousands and lasted far too many years?"

Several around us shift uncomfortably. Everyone here has lost many near and dear.

"What I'm about to tell you," Homer continues, "was told to me by a houseboy from King Agamemnon's household. Servants speak little but hear much as they fetch food and pour wine. And that is how he came to be near Agamemnon and his brother Menelaus on the day when Helen sailed for Troy. I believe the boy's words to be true. Judge for yourselves."

Jem and I lean against each other as the cool night breeze blows in from the sea.

"It started with shouting. Menelaus discovered that his not-so-loving wife had departed to warm the bed of Paris of Troy instead of his own. Menelaus' first words to his brother Agamemnon were ...

The bitch is on his boat!

She'll tire of him, Agamemnon said, *just as she did the others.*

The others were not princes in King Priam's golden hallways.

"And the moment that Menelaus uttered the word *golden*," Homer tells us, "Agamemnon sat up and focused his wine-soaked eyes."

I want Paris' pretty head, Menelaus said.

And I want his father's riches,
Agamemnon replied. *King Priam is old and
weak, soft from years without battles.*

*His trade with his neighbors has filled
his coffers with silver, gold, and gems.
They're ours for the taking.*

On what grounds? Menelaus asked. *Helen
left willingly, even eagerly.*

Oh, no, Agamemnon said through smiling
lips, *she was raped. And your dear wife
screamed - no, begged - for justice as
she left.*

You joke, but I want revenge.

And you'll have it, Agamemnon reassured
his brother.

But we'll also have Priam's treasures.

Homer breathes in the salty air of the
Aegean Sea, then gestures at the
hundreds of Greek ships that are lining
the coastline of Troy.

"And so our king set sail from Mycenae
and traveled to Athens, Mykonos, Delos,
Samos, then Crete - and to a dozen other
islands allied to Greece. Agamemnon
reassured them all:

The war will be brief, no more than a month. My army numbers 7,000, the largest in the Peloponnesus. Every tribe I've conquered, I've taken their best iron, their finest copper. Our spears are the sharpest, our swords, the strongest. Those who join us will return with their weight in gold. And the alliance you signed is quite clear: A wrong to one state is a wrong to us all.

"One by one, the island rulers were seduced as easily as if Helen herself had danced passionately in front of them wearing only chained gold coins. And so it began - the finest ships, the most noble of warriors, all assembled for the most ignoble of reasons."

Homer turns toward Jem and me and adds, "Perhaps our king of kings forgot that Priam's walled city has held all invaders at bay for a century."

CHAPTER 10: Corpse Masquerade

NARRATOR: JEM

At lunch, Three Toe and Two Blade are spitting olive pits at each other, pretending that death is an ocean away.

Two Blade grins, then says to me, "Ask him how he lost his toes."

"So how did you – "

Three Toe interrupts. "It's ancient history."

"Ahhh," teases Two Blade, "so it happened when you were a *baby?"*

Three Toe stuffs bread into his mouth and mumbles, "I barely remember."

Two Blade turns to me and jokes, "Prob'ly happened during battle. He must've gotten knocked in the head too."

Three Toe tosses a hard crust of bread at his friend's rather sizeable nose. It connects.

Two Blade is laughing, enjoying Three Toe's misery. "Was it glorious and noble? Were you saving a girl from certain death?"

Three Toe grins. "Definitely not glorious."

Two Blade cocks an eyebrow and reveals the real story. "He was stealing figs and dates from the back of a cart."

"And?" I ask.

"And he spooked the horse," Two Blade continues. "It reared up, then one of the cart wheels rolled over his big fat foot."

Three Toe's embarrassed. "No matter how much I screamed, that mare wouldn't move."

"And then the man who owned the cart came running," Two Blade says.

With an imaginary knife in hand, Three Toe shows me how he bent down and cut off his own toes to get away.

"Ouch!" I say. Even thinking about it hurts.

"He's been chased by Death himself, and he's outrun 'em all!" Two Blade says. "Except for once. *One* guy caught him."

"Yeah, but I was only twelve!" Three Toe protests.

"Ody caught 'im robbing his bedroom."

Two Blade is quite entertained by my reaction.

"Look at his face!" he roars. "Jem wants to know how the great Odysseus got stuck with such a lyin', thievin', toe-less, low-life in his regiment."

Three Toe grins. "He requested me."

"You're kidding?!" I say.

"Nope," Two Blade says. "Ody chooses men who refuse to die. They're the ones who are best at keeping each other alive."

Moments later, Odysseus joins us. "Did you like your hog-back bacon this morning?"

Two Blade points at his best buddy and deadpans, "It was so bad that he could only stomach five pieces."

Ody smiles. "I heard where we can get a lot more. Very reasonably priced."

Three Toe cocks an eyebrow. "Free?"

Ody nods.

"Trojan?" Two Blade asks.

Another nod.

Two Blade grins. "The best kind. I'm in."

"Me too," Three Toe says.

Ody points at Two Blade. "We're going to give that arm of yours another day to heal." Then he turns to me. "I could use a driver, Jem."

"Sure," I say, trying hard not to show how glad I am to be included in their little club. "When do we leave?"

"When do all scoundrels start work?" Two Blade asks.

"Nightfall," Ody says. "Eat first."

* * *

"So his name is Dolon, right?" Three Toe asks. "And he's a Trojan messenger."

Ody nods. "That's what our spies told me."

"What else do we know about him?" Three Toe asks.

Ody shrugs. "That he's not very bright, which is perfect, and that his one-horse chariot takes this same path every night. It's green."

I glance at the night sky and see little but clouds. Only a sliver of a moon is lighting this Trojan roadway. We're deep into enemy territory wearing dingy brown tunics that almost shout *We're from Greece!*

I'm nervous.

Instead of a chariot, we're crammed into a peasant's cart that's being pulled by the two worst nags in our stable. My nicknames for them are Slow and Slower.

Why these two? I asked Ody earlier.

Because we're going to sail *back.*

On our right is what used to be a forest. Even the tree roots have been ripped from the ground. Both sides constantly need wood for funeral pyres and campfires; finding it is becoming increasingly difficult as this war drags on.

There's a clear view of the Aegean Sea on our left. If we're attacked, at least we'll have a chance to outrun or out-swim the Trojans.

As we pass a pile of corpses that's twice Ody's height, I urge the horses to pick up the pace.

"*Perfect,*" Ody says. "Stop here."

Even Three Toe is surprised. "Here?!"

"We need to look Trojan, and these gentlemen," Ody points at the dead bodies, "would be glad to share their tunics with us."

"Maybe," Three Toe says anxiously, "they died of the plague."

Ody shakes his head. "No one wastes white shrouds on such men." Then he pulls a small body from the pile and rolls it toward me. "This one might be just right for you, Jem." He says this as if we're shopping at an agora in Athens.

Ody pulls hard on another corpse, then unrolls it from the soiled and spotted sheet surrounding it.

"And this guy," Ody jokes, "looks just like Dolon's cousin, don't you think?"

Neither Three Toe nor I have any idea what he's talking about.

Without even the slightest embarrassment, Ody strips, dons his "new" tunic, and wraps the dead man's burial garments around his shoulders. His bow and quiver of arrows are laying nearby.

"You're going to masquerade as a corpse?!" Three Toe says.

Ody grins. 'To live another day, I'll gladly hide among the dead at night."

All of us freeze as we hear a horse's hooves in the distance.

I squint. "Green chariot."

Ody smiles. "Right on schedule." He points at the area behind the pile of bodies. "Jem, keep our horses quiet." To Three Toe, he whispers, "Hide."

As the chariot approaches, Three Toe and I try not to move a muscle. The *not-too-bright* messenger, it seems, is far more relaxed.

He's whistling.

For Ody, it's show time.

Looking as if he's just crawled from Hades, the shrouded "corpse" staggers toward the middle of the path.

"Do-lon," he moans, "help me! I'm not dead yet!"

Three Toe and I exchange amused glances. Ody's performance seems a touch too theatrical for our tastes.

But it works!

The chariot stops. "Nathan! Is that you?!" Dolon steps onto the path.

The corpse stumbles toward "his cousin," then falls atop him.

Three Toe and I sprint toward the chariot. Dolon's shaking uncontrollably, certain that he's about to be added to the corpse pile.

Ody sits next to Dolon and begins a rather odd conversation. 'Relax, my friend. You're quite safe with us."

Dolon's eyes are the size of moons. He's not convinced that the three of us are here simply to chat.

"We're just looking for some bacon," Ody reassures him.

"Bacon?!" Dolon says.

"Well, pigs, to be specific," Ody says. "You drive past here almost every night, don't you?"

Dolon nods.

"And is tonight when the pig ship is due?"

Another nod.

"When?"

He points at the stars. "When Orion is at his height."

"Two-mast or three?'

"Three," Dolon answers, "but you'll smell it before you see it."

"Guarded?" Ody asks.

Dolon nods. "As if them pigs was gold."

"And where," Ody asks, "could we find a raft or a boat?"

"If I show you, you'll promise not to kill me?"

"Of course."

Dolon glances at Three Toe. "Him too?"

Ody nods. "I'm a man of my word."

And to my amazement, they shake hands.

"Bring your foot warmer along," Ody says.

Dolon lifts a large pottery urn from the base of his chariot and blows onto the embers to keep them glowing. We start toward the shoreline, but then Dolon rushes back to get five feet of rope and a smelly blanket from the chariot's storage compartment.

"We'll need these later," he says.

I haven't the slightest idea why we might want a short rope or a ratty horse blanket.

"Seven silvers for your foot warmer?" Ody says. "Is that fair?"

"More than fair," Dolon tells him, and exchanges the pottery urn for the money.

Surely we're not going to haul that astonishingly ugly thing back to our campsite?!

"And eight more for the row boat?" Ody asks.

"There are *four* rowing benches," Dolon says. "It's worth nine."

Ody nods. "And one more for your fine blanket?"

"Perhaps *two?"* Dolon says.

"Yes, of course, two," Ody says.

Three Toe and I can barely believe what we're hearing. The blanket is practically a rag. Ody's treating the guy more like a real cousin than a prisoner who has to do what we say.

We arrive at the shoreline and see the row boat that Dolon has assured us is *a fine craft.*

Three Toe kicks at the rotting wood on the moldy-yellow boat, then sits inside.

"It leaks," Three Toe complains.

"But only a little!" Dolon assures us.

Ody shrugs. "It will do."

Dolon pockets the handful of silvers, then rolls on the ground and wipes mud onto his face.

The evening just keeps getting weirder and weirder.

Dolon hands me his rope and says, "Okay, tie me up."

"Not too tight," Ody adds.

As I'm tying his wrists, Dolon explains. "I know Remus, the man who owns the boat. I'll pay him for it tomorrow morning. He'll untie me and verify my story."

"Your *story?*" Three Toe says.

"Yes," Dolon says with a snarl, "that a crazed *fat* man beat me and stole this boat." He's staring directly at Three Toe.

I try not to grin. Dolon is pushing his luck. He's the only man I've ever known who made money while being held captive.

In the distance we hear a steady drumbeat. And then words.

"Pull!" Drumbeat. "Pull!" Drumbeat. "Pull!" Drumbeat.

"The trireme will be here soon."

My eyes widen. Wren and I were taken from Lemnos on a trireme, then forced to board a three-mast ship. Scarp and Ukiah the Claw ran the entire operation.

"How many rowers?" Ody asks.

"Not even close to the normal two hundred," Dolon answers. "Maybe seventy-five."

Ody nods. "What about the lookout ship?"

"Twenty good rowers. Plus about thirty men with iron pikes."

"Forty-footers?'

Dolon nods. "All of the men with pikes are brutes. I've seen 'em push away a single-mast pirate ship so that no one could get close enough to board."

I swallow hard and try not to allow fear to rise in my stomach. A single iron pike could punch a hole in our rowboat and sink us.

"And the cargo ship?"

"The three-mast has a skeleton crew on board. It's depending on the trireme and the pike boat to keep raiders away."

"Do you know the captain?" Ody asks.

Dolon shakes his head. "He's new. Remus says he's mean. Has a claw instead of a right hand."

Ukiah the Claw is now working for the Trojans!

"Thanks," Ody says. "It's been a pleasure doing business with you."

"And you," Dolon says. He hesitates, then adds, "There's something else that might be important besides the pigs."

Ody wrinkles his forehead.

"*Bright seas*. Something called bright seas is on board the three-mast tonight, maybe in the cargo hold."

To my amazement, Ody pushes three more silvers into Dolon's pocket!

Three Toe snarls at Dolon. Dolon snarls back.

As we're pushing off from shore, I slip and fall.

"Ouch!"

"What's wrong?" Ody asks.

"Nothing." It was my own fault for not paying attention. *Bright seas* – I can't get those words out of my head.

"Let's see your foot," Ody says after we're all in the rowboat.

As I pull up my leggings, Ody's eyes tell me what I already know: I've sprained it badly.

"Brace yourself," he says, "this will hurt."

I don't allow myself to scream as Ody twists my ankle back into position.

But at that moment, my brain translates Dolon's final words.

"Briseis' sisters – *that's* what he really heard."

Ody nods.

As the three of us grab the oars, I'm trying not to think about the fact that one leaky rowboat is about to attack a trireme, a lookout boat equipped with iron pikes, as well as a three-mast ship.

And we're on a rescue mission.

I'm a little nervous.

CHAPTER 11: "Who's next to die?!"

NARRATOR: JEM

As we row into a channel of the Aegean Sea, Three Toe is grumbling after every pull on the oars.

"Next time you feel like giving away a pocketful of silvers, hand 'em to your *friends.*"

Ody grins. "If we see Dolon again, he'll be eager to do business."

"And I'm not *fat*, damn it!"

"Of course not." Ody leans back as he pulls on the oars. "Just big boned."

"We should throw his stinking blanket overboard!" Three Toe says.

Ody shakes his head. "We're going to need it. The urn too."

"It's ugly," Three Toe says. "Uglier even than this moldy boat."

"True," Ody says, then uses four arrows to stir the embers at the bottom of our seven-silver urn.

"You've got a *plan*, I hope," Three Toe says.

"Kind of."

"Kind of?!" Three Toe says.

"Keep rowing," Ody tells him.

"That's the plan?!"

Ody smiles. "For the moment, yes."

"Pull!" Drumbeat. *"Pull!"* Drumbeat. *"Pull!"*

A trireme has one purpose: to split an enemy ship in two and sink it. It's thin, lightweight for its size, and breathtakingly fast when two hundred slaves are rowing in unison.

Three Toe is staring at the sleek craft as it rounds a bend in the shoreline and comes fully into view.

"Iron blades. The best." There's tension in his voice.

A trireme has three tiers of oars. Below the water line is a massive battering ram as tall as a man. On each side of the ram as well as above it are iron blades. The highest blade is shaped like a dragon's head, and all sailors who see it know that soon they'll die.

"I don't think they've spotted us yet," Three Toe says softly.

Ody nods. "Get down, Jem. Cover yourself."

I reluctantly do as I'm told. Dolon's blanket is stinky. Really, *really* stinky. But it conveniently has several holes in it that allow me to peek through.

"Remus!" someone yells from the trireme. "Remus! Is that you?!"

I groan. All of the locals recognize this mold-covered rowboat. And all of them know the guy who owns it.

As always, Ody is thinking. He puts a finger to his lips, then points at the blanket covering me.

"Shhhh! You'll wake him."

After a long pause, we hear, "Who ... *are* ... you?!"

Ody again puts a finger to his lips. "Shhhh!"

"Halt or face death!"

"Row as if Hell is at our heels!" Ody whispers to Three Toe.

Three Toe begins turning our rowboat back toward the shore.

"*No*," Ody says, "get us between the trireme and the pike boat."

"That's crazy!"

"Trust me." Ody grabs the lion-skin grip on his long bow and removes one of four arrows from the pottery urn. Its iron tip is glowing and the head of the wooden shaft has tiny flames surrounding it.

Then we glide-glide-glide until the pike boat is on one side of us, the Trojan boat-ram on the other.

"Stop rowing," Ody says.

Three Toe's eyes are full of shocked disbelief.

"We're going to set the trireme on fire," Ody explains, then loads the arrow, aims, and fires. The shaft hits the mast.

"The breeze blew out the flames," Three Toe says.

"Damn!" Ody says softly.

The trireme commander bellows, "Ram the bastards!"

The drummer quickens his pace: boom*boom*boom*boom*.

"Ramming speed!" screams the commander.

Boom!Boom!Boom!Boom!

Three Toe tightens his hands on the oars. "I'm ready – whenever you say the word."

"Not yet," Ody says.

A dragon-shaped blade is aimed at the center of our rowboat. The trireme is moving with sickening speed. We'll be cut in two in fewer than a hundred heartbeats.

As Ody loads another arrow, I realize I can help.

"Wait!" I say. "Aim for the white phosphorus."

Ody's eyes flare. "Where?!"

"Back of the boat, last rowing position. It's in a huge urn on the top level."

Ody's eyes scan the ship. There's no direct path; we're too low and the third tier is too high.

"Up and over," suggests Three Toe. He moves his hand in an arc.

Ody nods, then strings the smoldering arrow.

Boom!Boom!Boom!Boom!

The arrow soars high, then falls somewhere onto the ship's highest level.

"The wind's from the east," Three Toe says softly. Hope has replaced panic in his voice.

The trireme's drumbeat is fast and loud: *Boom!Boom!Boom!Boom!*

Ody strings another arrow, then stares at the bulge on the side of Three Toe's belt. "You *always* stash bacon in your side pack."

"So?!" Three Toe says.

"Hog-back fat!"

Seconds later, Three Toe has coated more arrows with fat, Ody has shoved them into the urn, and I'm blowing on the embers.

"Flames!" I say.

"Finally!" Three Toe adds.

Ody balances himself on one knee, strains as he pulls on the long bow, and releases.

The flaming arc is magnificent.

"Fire on deck one," yells a man.

Another arrow is already ablaze with blue and yellow flames. Ody loads the burning shaft, pulls until his fingers risk being singed, and releases it.

The trireme is nearly on top of us. From its highest deck, we hear men jumping from their rowing positions and running.

"Row, damn you, row!" screams the trireme commander.

Another arrow is now in place. With no hesitation, Ody launches our last chance.

Flaming Death soars high above the trireme, then begins its descent.

The huge orange and black pottery urn on Scarp's trireme held at least fifty pitcherfuls of white phosphorus. I'm hoping this ship is identical.

"White fire!" shouts one of the sailors. "Run!"

Ody and I exchange smiles.

The drumbeat ceases. Men atop the trireme are running wildly toward the ship's bow.

Ody pulls on one oar so that our rowboat is facing the same direction as the trireme. We're now a slightly smaller target.

The urn of white phosphorus explodes, showering the trireme's top level and most of the men with its flaming white paste.

Their screams sicken me as they leap overboard. Despite the water, their hair, shirts, and pants remain on fire. Once aflame, white phosphorus is notoriously hard to put out.

The battering ram misses us, but the trireme's portside collides with our side timbers.

And our small leak becomes a large one.

"Row for the three-mast," Ody says. "Jem, start bailing water."

For the second time, the ugly pottery urn is proving to be quite valuable, easily worth Ody's seven silvers.

"All hands to starboard! All hands to starboard!" The voice from the pike boat is frantic. I turn and see why.

Every man on the deck has a forty-foot pike balanced atop the railing. Their desperate eyes tell me that they know what's about to happen.

"Shove it aside, mates! Shove it aside!"

Thirty iron pikes are positioned as the trireme approaches. But thirty men are not enough to push away a craft built to hold two hundred oarsmen.

The dragon's tongue is a sharp-tipped shaft of bronze. It easily punches through the hull of the pike boat. On the deck, its men continue grunting, giving their all.

But it's already too late.

Iron blades are slicing into the pike boat, splintering the starboard timbers. It sounds like lightning splitting a tree.

The trireme's flaming sail is lighting up the night sky. As the two ships collide, the trireme's mast collapses and its sail falls, setting both ships ablaze.

For anyone on the top deck, escape is now impossible.

"Don't look," Ody tells us as he pulls on his oars. "Focus on the three-mast."

Despite my frantic efforts at bailing, we're taking on far too much water. Ody sees the panic in my eyes. He points at my swollen ankle. "Can you swim?"

"Maybe."

He knows I'm lying.

He takes my trembling shoulders in his hands and with surprising calm looks me in the eye. "I will not let you die. Understand?"

I nod.

As our boat sinks, Ody rips the blanket into long strips, ties the oars together, then says, "We can float on these." In truth, *we* means me.

Ody points at the three-mast and smiles. "Soon we'll own that ship.' Three Toe and I are almost crazy enough to believe him.

Our always-optimistic leader pulls his quiver of arrows and his long bow over his chest. Then the three of us slide into the water and begin frog-kicking.

All of us are shivering when we finally reach the side of what Dolon called *the pig boat*. We grab its anchor, which is hoisted just above the waterline.

"How many men on board?" whispers Three Toe.

"Skeleton crew," Ody says. "Maybe ten men."

Three Toe actually grins. "It's almost too easy. I'll take the stern."

Ody nods. 'Right, divide and conquer. And we have a big advantage."

He sees the amazement on my face.

"They think we're dead."

Three Toe grabs the thick anchor rope and silently begins climbing it.

"Lash that sail to the mast, damn you!" shouts one of the men on the deck.

"I've got me own troubles!" says another. "Do it yerself!"

"Hang onto my belt," Ody whispers. "We've going to the other end."

With powerful strokes, Ody swims to the front of the ship, then he shows me that some of the beams are rough-hewn enough so that I can find a hand-hold.

Seconds later, he's thrashing about, sounding like a drowning man.

"'elp me, mate! 'elp!"

"I see yah!" someone on deck says.

As the man throws down a long rope ladder, I see that his forearm is tattooed with the octopus symbol that identifies one of the Damnati.

"Grab the pole!" he shouts, then dangles the smooth end of a pike.

He's just offered Ody a quick, easy way to kill him.

Ody seizes the iron pole with both hands, anchors his feet against the ship's belly, and thrusts himself back into the waves. And with him he drags another of Scarp's scum. The hook end of the pike is buried deeply in the man's shoulder and the heavy weight quickly sends him to the bottom.

Ody surfaces, grabs the end of the rope ladder, and begins his climb. I follow.

As we peek over the deck railing, I notice Three Toe creeping along the starboard quarter. He pulls his slingshot from his belt, loads it with a lead ball, swings and releases.

Whack! Direct hit to a deckhand's forehead.

"Two down, eight to go," I mutter.

In the distance we hear the roaring of fire and the hissing of steam as the timbers of the trireme break apart and sink.

Ody and I crouch behind several coiled ropes. "Wait here," he tells me. "If you have to, sneak below and hide with the animals."

Moments later, he's disappeared into the shadows.

On the deck, a man dressed in all black crawls from the lower hull. "I see you!" he roars at Three Toe.

It's Ukiah the Claw. His beard is matted, his hair unwashed. Two men soon join him.

Instead of running, Three Toe shouts, "Where are Briseis' sisters?!"

"You, you're their rescuer?!" Ukiah is laughing as he straps a sword blade onto his forearm. "I tired of them days ago and sold the pair to Agamemnon. He paid a fine price."

Despite the fact that the slingshot in his hand is unloaded, Three Toe is moving slowly toward the Claw.

Ukiah smiles. "There's nothing I enjoy more than handing so-called *heroes* their own heads."

He motions for his men to stand aside. They obey.

Three Toe's eyes tell me that he welcomes the challenge.

"Is this sorry excuse for a man a *pygmy*?" Ukiah asks his lieutenants. "Or is he one of Zeus' *turds* that's fallen from the heavens?"

His men laugh. Three Toe is stone faced.

"You were the runt of the litter, weren't you, boy?" Ukiah says tauntingly. "It's amazing your mother didn't drown you before you opened your eyes."

Even though Ukiah towers over him, I don't see even a hint of fear in Three Toes' eyes.

"Short, stupid, and ugly – what woman would want such a man?"

But the abuse stops suddenly. Ukiah the Claw is astonished to see a silver blade in the center of his right foot. And as he screams, another hidden blade appears from underneath Three Toe's belt. A second later, its shaft is buried inside the Claw's open mouth.

Ukiah's name calling has been replaced with the sound of gurgling blood. He lurches forward and falls.

The Claw is now at the feet of the man he mocked. His final sight is of Three Toe standing high above him.

Ukiah's men begin moving toward Three Toe simultaneously. One is swinging a bludgeon; the other is slicing the air with a curved-blade saber.

Before the first man can release his weapon, one of Ody's arrows enters his heart.

THUD!

The second man's head hits the deck as his legs are pulled out from under him. A heartbeat later, his sword is in Three Toe's hands.

"Who's next to die?!" shouts someone near the center mast.

Ody! I look up and see that his knife is pressed against a throbbing vein on a sailor's neck.

"No volunteers?" Ody smiles. "Wise decision. Can all of you swim?"

The remaining sailors nod nervously.

"Then you'll live to tell your wives about an amazing day." Ody points to the portside. Moments later, they're swimming for shore.

I shake my head in wonder. We were outnumbered more than three-to-one, yet the ship is now ours.

Three Toe is howling with laughter. *"Who's next to die?!"*

Ody grins. "Well, it worked, didn't it?"

We begin searching the lower-deck to make sure that none of Ukiah's men are still onboard. The last cabin is locked.

"Seen any keys," Three Toe asks.

"None," I answer. "We'll never be able to break those chains."

Ody examines the iron links with a lantern. "Nope, never."

Then he destroys the bottom hinge with a single kick and rips the door from its frame.

"No, no!" screams a terrified girl. Behind her is someone smaller, obviously her sister.

Ody's eyes widen. "Briseis asked us to find you. You have my word that you will not be harmed."

* * *

By morning, we're docking at the same area where Wren and I landed a week ago.

Thump!

The anchor drops.

"We come bearing gifts," Ody bellows to the curious men on the shoreline. "Come help us unload."

I limp toward the hatch that leads to the cargo hold, then help Three Toe open it. The stench is overwhelming but the sounds coming from below are almost musical.

Quack, quack, quack.

Oink! Oink-oink-oink!

A sailor helps us lower the ramp from the cargo hold, then stares in amazement. "Look at all of them *beaut-i-ful* pigs."

We nod.

"That, lads," he says smiling broadly, "is the smell of *bacon*."

CHAPTER 12: "As soon as I can find a raft."

NARRATOR: WREN

A three-mast ship with a midnight-blue rag for a flag docks at our port.

"We come bearing gifts," shouts a man from the top of the tallest mast.

Ody's back!

People on shore begin gathering as Jem and Three Toe open the cargo hold. A long ramp is lowered, and pig after pig after pig stumbles from the ship to land. The sight is glorious.

Fifty men rush aboard and begin unloading more chicken cages than I've ever seen before.

"Eggs!" one of the men screams. "They've brought *eggs!*"

Last off the huge ship are Briseis' two sisters and its only crew: Three Toe, Ody, and Jem – who's riding atop Ody's shoulders. As my twin is lowered onto the sand, I see that his right ankle is badly swollen.

Everyone's shouting, overwhelmed with emotions as we hug each other. It's part joy, part amazement.

"How," I ask, "did you capture a three-mast?!"

"That?!" Three Toe says as he glances over his shoulder. "*That* hunk of junk was nothing. Sinking the other two boats was what made us sweat. Jem blew up the trireme – *a*-maz-ing sight!"

"Jem?!" I say with more-than-a-little doubt in my voice. He blushes.

"Ody helped a bit," Three Toe says with a wink.

Odysseus takes me aside, then bends onto one knee and looks me in the eye.

"You know how much we need horses."

I nod.

"We learned last night where the Trojans have a stable."

I grin. "And you're going to steal every one of them."

Ody nods. "But I need someone who's good with stallions, someone who can keep them quiet. Will you help me?"

"Can my brother come too?"

Ody points at Jem's ankle. "He's been through a lot. He needs to rest."

"When do we leave?" I ask.

"As soon as I can find a raft."

"A raft?!" Three Toe says.

Ody nods. "We'll float there, ride back. Are you with me?"

"Always!" Three Toe says.

"Good. Go tell that lay-about Two Blade that he'll have to earn his supper today."

* * *

Dysendra brings us water skins, hog-back bacon, lots of hard-boiled eggs, and three bags filled with carrots - bribes for the stolen stallions, not us.

The raft has a crude sail rigged onto a makeshift mast as well as a couple of twenty-foot barge poles that Three Toe, Ody, and Two Blade will use to muscle our way past eddies and rough currents. Animal hides are piled onto one edge of the raft to help us with the nighttime cold. Finally, there are four large coils of rope, enough for the four of us to tie the horses together and lead them away.

* * *

Nine hours later, the sun is setting and we're getting edgy as we think about all of the details we need to know but don't. Ody strains his eyes, searching the shoreline for the landmarks that someone named Dolon assured him would be here.

"How much longer?" Two Blade asks.

"Soon," Ody says.

"We're losing the light," Three Toe complains.

"What if Dolon lied about the guards?" Two Blade says nervously. "We could be walking into a trap."

"No," Ody says firmly. "Dead men deliver no bribes. Dolon wants us alive so we can bring him more of our silver. He said there'd be three guards, only one when they're eating, and I believe him."

Three Toe grunts as he uses the barge pole to push us into the center of the current. "As soon as we ask someone, *Hey, are the stables around here?*, we're dead."

His point is a good one. They'll be suspicious of strangers.

Everyone but Two Blade is wearing the clothes Ody stripped off of the Trojan corpses last night. I've got on the same tunic that Jem wore, and it's far too big for me.

Ody is strangely silent, then he breathes a sigh of relief. "We're here."

Three Toe and I exchange doubtful glances. The twilight is making it hard to see anything distinctly, and the terrain in front of us looks little different from what we've seen for most of the afternoon.

"You can see the stables from here," Ody says.

At first I think he's joking. With the exception of two trails, there's nothing man-made for as far as the eye can see. Then the wind shifts and my nose confirms Ody's words. I smell hay and horses.

Three Toe is bewildered. *"Stables?"*

"There," Ody says, glancing at the shoreline.

"There?!" Three Toe says, seeing nothing.

I nudge him and point upwards. *"There."*

It's a twenty-foot-high ridge. The side is covered with vines and roots in sandy soil. The horses are mostly fenced in by natural barriers.

We float a bit further downstream, drag our raft onto the shore, then double-back with coils of rope on our backs and sacks of carrots in our hands.

"Dolon said we'll surprise them if we climb up the vines," Ody says.

Three Toe, the smallest of the men, grabs a handful of roots, pulls, and falls on his butt. Two Blade clamps a hand over his mouth to keep from laughing.

On the west side is a path covered with horse tracks, but there's no doubt in my mind that guards would meet us on the other end.

I test my weight against the vines and roots on the hillside. They hold.

"I'll climb it," I suggest, "and count the guards."

Ody hesitates. "It's risky."

"You smell the meat?" Two Blade asks. "They're eating."

Three Toe nods. "One guard."

Ody turns to me. "If anyone stops you, say Dolon sent you. Tell them he was robbed and needs a horse."

It's not much of a plan, but it's the best one we've got at the moment. So I begin my climb, pausing often as my hands search for tree roots instead of vines.

After I reach the top of the ridge, I find a grove of trees, so I continue climbing. The tallest branches allow me to see inside their campsite.

Two large men are huddled near a fire. A third is probably no older than sixteen, and he has a nasty cough that allows me to know where he is every few seconds.

But what takes my breath away are fifty fine stallions. Soon they'll be ours.

"They said he'd be here to change horses by nightfall," says one of the guards.

"Who cares?"

"*I* care. I've never met somebody like that. He'll prob'ly be wearing *purple*."

"They squat and piss just like you and me. And I don't like being ordered around by some fool who thinks I should cook him supper."

"This one's different. He wins battles."

"Lies. None of 'em fight. They say they do, but they don't."

I descend cautiously. If I fall, they'll know we're here, and then we'll never get those magnificent horses.

My grin tells almost the whole story as I touch the ground.

"Stallions?" Ody asks.

I nod. "No plow horses, no nags! One kid at the front gate, two big guys who aren't done eating."

"Good, we'll finish it for them," Two Blade says. He and Three Toe grin like kids.

"And there's one more thing," I say.

Ody kneels, giving me his complete attention.

"They're expecting someone important soon, someone royal. He'll want a fresh horse."

Ody smiles. "Perfect."

Three Toe pulls his slingshot from his belt. "I could sneak up the pathway first, then drop the guard with one shot."

"Excellent," Ody says.

"Double-ball him to make sure," Two Blade says. "We don't want him warning the others."

Three Toe turns to Ody. "And then we rush 'em?"

"No. We'll make them come to us."

"How?" Two Blade asks.

"Trust me," Ody says.

"And what about me?" I ask.

"You'll stay here," Ody answers. "We'll bring the horses down to you."

"And if someone comes?" I ask.

Two Blade attempts a high-pitched voice. *"I work for Dolon."*

Three Toe is already creeping up the horse trail. His slingshot is loaded. Thirty paces behind, Two Blade and Ody follow; both are carrying coils of rope.

Cough-cough-cough-cough-cough.

The youngest guard belongs in bed.

Th-wock!

A lead ball connects with his skull. He's going to wake up with a huge headache.

Thud!

His body hits the ground.

And Ody calls out rather grandly, "His lordship has arrived!"

The two guards come running at full speed.

THUMP!

A body flies from the ridge and tumbles over the roots we were testing our weight on only moments ago.

WHOMP!

And then a second.

Two Blade and Three Toe are good men to have around when you want to kill people quickly. They're a little weak on doing it quietly.

Ody leads ten horses down the pathway. He's rushing them. The dappled stallion is making a lot more fuss than I'm comfortable with.

"Easy, fella. It's all right." I buy his silence with a carrot.

"Gotta hurry," Ody mutters, then sprints up the pathway.

I tie the lead horse to one of the roots at the bottom of the cliff. But if he decides to fight me, he'll break free and we'll lose the entire group.

At the top of the ridge, I hear Two Blade cussing at the horses. I should be up there, not him.

I'm on edge as Three Toe brings down ten more horses, two with bridles on them.

"A champion like you deserves a carrot," I say to the wary lead stallion, then tie the group to the thickest root I can find.

Maybe this will work. Maybe the Trojans are just as short of healthy guards as the Greeks are.

But then I hear it: marching, two men in unison. I grab a rag from my pocket and pretend to be grooming the Appaloosa.

The Trojan guards see me and halt.

"You recognize 'er?"

The older one shakes his head.

"You!" the man with missing teeth says, "You don't belong here!"

"I work for *his lordship*, not you!" I say, desperately hoping that my lie will buy me some time. "He wants these stallions in Troy by morning!"

They hesitate. Then the one with the bad teeth spots the two guards with broken necks.

"You're coming with us!"

"Ody!" I try to shout, but a heartbeat later I'm facedown in the sand with my breath knocked out of me.

One of them kicks me in the head so hard that I almost pass out.

"Scream again, you little bitch, and you'll lose a few teeth." His face is an inch from mine; his breath sickens me.

I hear horses galloping toward us.

"She'll fetch a fine price in the slave market," one of my captors says.

A woman's voice shouts, "That girl is no one's slave!"

The man standing above me turns and snarls. "This knife says the girl is ours."

But the older guard stiffens almost as if Death has him by the throat. "Sir, we ... we ...."

The woman lifts me into their chariot. "You'll be safe with us."

As the horses bolt away, I hear the quarreling guards' final words.

"He's only one man!"

"That's *Hector*, you fool!"

CHAPTER 13: Hector, Helen, a New Home

Six days later

NARRATOR: WREN

I remember little about the delirious chariot ride back to Troy except the sound of a crying baby and fragments of conversation.

The peasants need my help. They're hungry and desperate for medicine. The countryside is no longer safe.

It's gotten that bad?

Worse. Pirates have stolen the wheat shipment from Cypress. Soon we'll be starving too.

The side of my face where the guard kicked me is still swollen, but I'm no longer seeing double or feeling dizzy. And I've convinced Andra and Hector that I'm better with horses than babies. Their son isn't even a year old yet.

I hate to lie, but I've done a lot of it during the past few days. Supposedly I know little about the war and nothing about men named Achilles, Agamemnon, and Odysseus. I'm an orphan from Lemnos who has worked in the stables since I was four.

My biggest lie is the one I haven't said out loud. Nobody here knows that I have a twin who works day and night to keep the Greek war horses healthy enough so that they can be ridden into battle.

Much of what I thought I knew about Troy is what King Agamemnon wanted me to believe. And everything I believed about Hector, who's killed more Greek soldiers than any other Trojan, was wrong.

He's awesomely strong, but he's not the brute I expected him to be. My bedroom is next to Hector and Andra's, and each morning I hear his prayers.

Father Zeus, keep my eyes clear. May I never harm the helpless or strike the unarmed. Lord Apollo, guide my hands. Let each blow be honorable.

Goddess Athena, grant me wisdom, never glory.

Protect my wife. Save my son.

Five days ago, I awoke to find him hovering above me. His eyes were filled with relief.

Good, your fever is gone.

Where am I?

In Priam's palace. You are safe here, and welcome. I've brought you bread and figs, some goat's milk too. Can you sit up?

I don't know why, but I couldn't stop looking at the cup he was drinking from, which was identical to mine.

What's puzzling you, Wren?

Your cup. It's tin.

Hector smiled.

So?

I thought that gold was everywhere in Troy.

You'd make my father laugh. Before this horrible war, we kept the seas free of pirates and guaranteed safe passage for

all merchants. And for that, we were given a great deal of gold and silver. There's now little left of it in the royal vaults.

But how?!

Mercenaries. Wheat from Cyprus. Wood from Turkey. The walls around this fortress keep us safe, but everything we eat must be smuggled past the Greeks. The bribes are endless.

But nothing has amazed me more than to see how beautiful Helen of Troy truly is. Or to learn how far she's fallen. Her new husband is Paris, Hector's younger brother. Just last evening, I overheard the three of them arguing in the hallway.

Hector was returning from the battlefield, bloody and sweaty. Paris and Helen, perfumed and smiling, were leaving their bedroom.

How can I send my men into battle when the man who set it all in motion is afraid to fight?

I'm fit for finer things than hacking at filthy Greeks.

Then Paris stormed away. Disgusted, Hector turned to Helen.

You left a daughter in Greece. You were married to a prince there. Wasn't that enough?!

All that is past.

I cringed as she touched his arm.

But you and I, oh yes, we could have a future.

Hector backed up a step.

I am not one of your houseboys who can be so easily tempted.

Helen's face hardened.

Don't begrudge me my one weakness. Men are playthings. I tease, I tempt, I trouble their minds. They're the only amusement I have inside this suffocating palace.

You shame my brother - and yourself - daily.

A war was started so that the two of you could be together.

You're the man I wanted; he's the man I could get. And now that I have him, he bores me. As does this war.

She moved closer, speaking just above a whisper.

I pray daily that your spears will find their way to Achilles' heart.

Your charms are wasted on me.

And her smile disappeared.

CHAPTER 14: Into Battle

NARRATOR: JEM

"Companies, assemble!" shouts one of the heralds. The huge gates that separate our tents from the battleground are being pulled open by two oxen.

It's been very, very hard not to think about Wren. Everyday I drive Three Toe and Two Blade's chariot to the battlefield and they compete for kills as if it's a game.

After every Trojan falls, I imagine that he's someone who tried to harm Wren. Last night I dreamed that she returned to our camp by walking over a path made of their dead corpses.

Three Toe, Two Blade, and I have an unspoken agreement: none of us is allowed to say *I wonder if she's safe*. Every morning we go onto the battlefield. And each night we return, so exhausted that we grab something to eat, then fall into bed.

Sometimes the white sands are almost covered with red blood. The combat zone is basically a slaughterhouse.

But even so, there are unwritten rules that the soldiers on both sides follow. One, treat the chariot drivers as if they're invisible. And two, don't aim for the horses – they didn't start this war.

It's strange: you re scum if you kill a horse, yet you're a hero for bringing home forty Trojan helmets.

"Will Achilles fight today?" asks one of the soldiers who's falling into place behind us.

Two Blade shakes his head.

Agamemnon hasn't returned Briseis, so Achilles and the legion of Spartans who've pledged themselves to him still aren't on the battlefield.

"Each day they get bolder," Three Toe complains.

They means the Trojans, the Turks too. The Turkmen in the nearby villages have been volunteering to fight against us. They know they'll be the next to die if Agamemnon sacks Troy.

The Trojans and Turks are fighting for their families and their farms. We're fighting so that our king of kings can grow fatter and add piles of gold to his treasury.

"Without Achilles, we'll lose," I mumble. Everybody thinks it, but nobody says it. The size of our funeral pyres has been growing every day.

Three Toe stiffens. The words I've spoken are treasonous. Men have been whipped to within an inch of their lives for saying less.

"If Agamemnon would step aside, Ody could get us past those Trojan walls."

More treason, this time it's from Two Blades' lips.

"How?" Three Toe asks.

"The man's a trickster like no other," Two Blade says. "He'd find a way."

The oxen finish opening the gates. "Good," I say. "We're finally moving."

There are a thousand men in front of us and at least four thousand more behind. Hundreds will die today. Hundreds more will be wounded.

"Jem!" comes a thunderous voice from nearby.

It's Ajax, the only warrior whose chariot is driverless. Once he steps onto its platform, there's barely enough room for even a mouse – a small one – to stand.

I turn. He's smiling broadly.

"Send a few fools who are eager to die my way. Don't let Three Toe have all the glory."

"I'll try," I say with a grin.

"Good lad."

Some call Ajax *The Wall* because of his size.

They're wrong. He's a mountain.

I'm jittery as the blood-stained battleground comes into view. But truthfully, if there's anyone who's going to live to see tomorrow, it's me.

After King Agamemnon decreed that all stable boys must join the fight, Ody protected me. He personally gave the order that I'd be the driver for Three Toe and Two Blade. Then he put us behind the phalanx, which is the closest thing the Greek army has to a death machine.

Sixteen men wide, sixteen men deep – more than a hundred and fifty fighters in a tightly packed square. Their spears are unusually long, about thirty hand lengths. Six men handle each spear, all of them thrusting at the same time. At first glance the Trojans see no men, only shields and endless shafts of metal, each of which ends in a jagged bronze blade that will tear them apart.

Awake or asleep, it's the same: when I close my eyes, I see the blood and dismembered body parts that this meat grinder leaves behind.

Nothing gets past a phalanx.

"For Athens!" some of the soldiers shout as their horses charge toward the Trojans.

"For Sparta!"

"For Crete!"

My jaws are clamped shut. Lemnos is gone, burned to nothingness by men working for Agamemnon, the king of kings, bastard of all bastards.

The sun is shining brightly this morning, but our chariot is in the shade of a large tree – or, to be more accurate, we're in the shadow of Ajax's oak shield, which is strapped onto his back.

His shield is half of a hollowed-out tree trunk. He must have searched for a long time to find the right one, because he – and his tree – are beyond huge. There's no crest, no engraving on the front, just the countless cuts from sword blades that have tried to hack their way through it. The bottom begins at Ajax's toes and the top extends a few inches above his bushy black hair.

"To hell with this!" Ajax bellows impatiently, then steers his chariot to the left. Seconds later, his horses are galloping toward a pathway that's one of the Trojans' favorites.

Three Toe and Two Blade exchange glances. Both grin.

"Tired of following the sausage maker?" Three Toe asks me.

I nod, then tug on our chariot's reins. My horses charge past the phalanx.

Ajax is second only to Achilles in his ability to halt an enemy surge. Yet he's rarely blood-soaked at the end of each day. No one fights like Ajax. *No one.*

He stops, dismounts, then turns his horses so that they won't see the Trojans rushing toward us. I follow his lead. Nothing about our two chariots marks them as being Greek or Trojan.

Next Ajax positions his "tree" near the chariot pathway but not inside it.

"Bring me hammer, will yah lads?"

Three Toe reaches inside Ajax's chariot, grabs the triple-braided leather loop connected to the handle, and grunts as he heaves it toward Two Blade, who grabs it with both hands and drags it until it's next to the "tree."

"Solid iron," Ajax says, answering the question that my face has written all over it.

"And the handle?"

"Granite."

The hammer's head is as big as the largest Trojan's helmet. The handle is thicker than Two Blade's arm.

A horde of enemy chariots is charging toward us. We're not their target. They're hoping to hit a column of Greek fighters from the side. Ajax is going to slow them down.

A lot.

But within a hundred heartbeats, the Trojans will be here.

"Hurry," I urge Ajax.

He raises an eyebrow. "No need, lad, no need."

Three Toe smiles, then whispers, "The man's not made for speed."

It's true that Ajax can't really run, but his hands are awesomely fast when they need to be, which our enemies are about to find out.

The ground is shaking as all of us take our positions behind Ajax's shield.

As the first Trojan chariot passes us, the giant's right arm shoots out.

CLANG!

Ajax's granite hammerhead connects with a Trojan helmet. And the soldier collapses, just as dead as if one of the gods had slammed him against a mountain side.

Two Blade grabs a passing Trojan's chest plate and pulls *hard*.

WHAM! The base of his double-bladed ax crushes the side of the man's helmet.

CLANG! WHAM! *CLANG!* WHAM! *CLANG!* WHAM!

The process repeats itself again. And again. And again. The stack of bodies grows.

Three Toe, our *one-shot-drops-'em-every-time* slinger is unleashing his lead balls at a furious rate.

"Catch!" he yells. And another Trojan falls.

"Eat *this*, scum suckers!"

Two "rocks" fly from his slingshot. Two riders thud to the ground.

And then a truly astonishing sight unfolds.

Three Toe nudges Two Blade. "Pile up!"

"Oh yeah!" his buddy says with a grin.

The seemingly unstoppable column of Trojans has not just been slowed, it's been halted and thrown into a state of chaos. Several of their chariots have collided with each other. Dozens of men are trying to crawl free from the wreckage.

CLANG! WHAM! *CLANG!* WHAM!

Ajax and Two Blade are slamming their weapons against the chest plates and helmets of the downed men. Their deaths are quick and bloodless.

Ajax grabs a corpse by its feet, then swings the body like a club, knocking solider after soldier off his stallion.

From inside the pileup we hear cries of intense pain.

"Lord Soros is hurt!"

"The prince! The prince!"

Two Blade approaches the heavily armored man. A torn royal-purple sash is caught between his helmet and chest plate.

"His neck!" yells another man.

One glance at the twisted angles of the man's body tells us everything we need to know. Lord Soros' neck is broken and he'll never walk again.

Two Blade is standing over him.

"Kill me!" begs the prince. "End this now!"

The blunt end of Two Blade's ax crushes the side of the dying prince's helmet. The shrieking ends.

The prince's attendant kneels at Two Blade's feet and assumes the position of the supplicant.

"We plead for your mercy." His entire body is trembling. "And we beg for safe passage of the body back to his father."

"Granted."

"Safe passage! Safe passage for the prince!" shouts a herald.

A hundred chariots turn back toward Troy.

CHAPTER 15: Riding the Death Ram

NARRATOR: WREN

Servants have just finished wiping the rainwater from the benches in the amphitheater where all major ceremonies are held. To everyone's relief, the storm that howled all last night finally seems to have ended.

As we enter, I'm surrounded by members of the royal family. Hector and Andra are allowing me to hold their baby son and they're treating me as if I'm a member of the family.

I'm touched, and very, very grateful.

I'm sitting between Helen of Troy and Andra of the House of Hector. Usually they're respectful to one another even though they dislike each other intensely.

Helen has wine on her breath this morning. Not good.

The crowd is hushed as King Priam enters the amphitheater. Dressed in a black tunic, he's riding his favorite horse, a white Arabian. As a guard hands him a torch, Priam holds his head high.

How can any man, royal or common, prepare himself to do what must be done today? His subjects — everyone in this arena — expect him to show strength, to be unflinching and stoic.

But how can any father not have tears flowing down his face as he sets fire to the body of his youngest son?

Soros died yesterday, his neck broken as he charged into battle.

Priam dismounts and walks toward the three-tiered wooden tower at the center of the arena.

One touch of the torch to the funeral pyre is all that's really necessary, but tradition dictates that all three levels must be set afire. The highest level, where Prince Soros' body is, is barely within Priam's reach.

As the king lifts the torch, he steps back for no more than a second, inhales deeply, then continues spreading the flames that will soon surround his son.

"He won't last much longer," Helen whispers to Paris. She's smiling. Priam's pain is her amusement.

Andra stiffens as she overhears the comment. She suspects, as I do, that Helen fancies herself to be the next queen. Helen is conveniently ignoring the fact that Hector is next in the line of succession, not Paris.

As the flames rise higher and higher, Andra sobs. Helen is unmoved.

After horns sound sad, low notes, the crowd begins to leave. We rise.

"Let's finish that wine," Paris whispers to Helen.

Helen nods. "An excellent plan."

Prince Soros' widow turns to confront Helen. "My husband fought daily, as does Hector, yet Paris has never made even a ceremonial appearance on the battlefield."

Helen is staring contemptuously as if her sister-in-law is beneath her. "Troy needs my husband's wisdom more than it needs his blood. Soros was a fool; Paris is not."

Several people around us gasp in disbelief. Helen seems to think that she has no need for kindness or tact since she has beauty. And if Paris inherited any shrewdness, I've never seen him show it.

Andra is red-faced with anger. "So Hector is a *fool* to be fighting for our survival - and yours?!"

Helen half-hides her drunken giggles. "Perhaps Hector's destiny is to die on the battlefield. And perhaps mine is to be Troy's queen."

Andra's face hardens. "This kingdom could not survive with Paris as its head."

"Then we're all doomed, aren't we?" Helen laughs. "How tragic." She turns and walks away.

"It must be convenient to have a second home in Greece," someone whispers.

How true.

* * *

The stables here are far larger than my father's were, so simply bringing oats and fresh hay to each of the horses sometimes takes two hours. From the windows, I've been watching King Priam, who's sometimes riding, sometimes walking beside his stallion.

The things that I overheard at the funeral are still troubling me. Some men should never be kings. Agamemnon is one such man. Paris is another. With Helen by his side, their palace would shine but Troy itself would crumble.

King Priam is a simple, honest man who has no patience with attendants who grovel at his feet or want to throw robes over his shoulders. He's ordered me to never bow when he enters the stables.

As I'm filling a feeding bin with more oats, he greets me with a compliment.

"The horses have thrived under your care, Wren."

"Thank you."

As he hands me the reins of his Arabian, I notice he's trembling. He's scary-thin, and breakfast was many hours ago.

"Please rest for a moment." He allows me to hold his arm as I lower him onto a wooden stool.

"Let me get you something to eat."

"No!" he says with surprising emotion. "Every bite I eat is one that I'm stealing from the mouths of our soldiers."

"But you're not well."

"I'm well enough."

His eyes are fixed on a blood-red pennant that's flying from an all black mast in the harbor: Achilles' ship.

"Someday they'll meet in battle," King Priam says.

"Achilles and Hector?"

He nods. "May the gods strike me dead before that day comes. I could not bear to lose my eldest son, and this kingdom must not lose its next king."

Priam rises slowly, then runs his right hand along his old horse's still graceful neck. "No extra oats for this one, Wren. He'll never see battle. And no double rations for Paris' pretty ponies. The fat on their haunches should embarrass my second son. Unfortunately, nothing does."

He sighs and leaves.

This man, not Agamemnon, deserves to be called the king of kings. But he'd laugh at the title, then order that those words never be uttered again.

* * *

As sunset nears, I'm outside the stables running one of the horses through her daily routine. From high atop Dancer, I see Hector approaching. Something is on his mind.

He smiles and greets my horse first.

"Ah, Dancer, you're such a lucky lady." He turns to me. "I can always tell your favorites. Just your voice soothes them. They'll do anything for you."

I blush. "And I'd do anything for them. Dancer, Dauntless, Ever-strong, and Thunderhoof, they're my best."

"And that's why I'd like to borrow them tonight."

I nod.

Hector points to the shoreline. "Last night's rain did more than wash my brother's blood from the battlefield. The trench that the Greeks worked so hard to dig is now worthless. The storm surge filled it with sand and mud."

"So our chariots can roll over the unguarded areas?"

Hector nods. "And the winds weakened their wall. If we can break through it, our archers could set half their ships on fire."

I dismount from my horse and walk with Hector into the stables.

He lowers his voice and asks, "You've heard about the pirates?"

"They stole the wheat shipment from Crete."

Hector nods. "And the one from Delos. Soon we'll be starving."

I'm shocked. I had no idea that the situation was this bad.

"Our spies say that Achilles is still refusing to fight. And we have a new weapon that they will not expect. That's why I want to attack the Greeks tonight."

"The new weapon, is it what your men hid in the stables two nights ago?"

Hector wrinkles his forehead. "You miss nothing, do you? Its builder calls it the Death Ram."

"It has harness rings for forty horses."

"Two by two, ten deep," Hector says. "The rail in the middle separates the teams."

"There's only room for one rider atop the seat on that rail."

He nods.

"No one can control forty horses."

"You could, if your four led the others."

I stop walking, stunned by the enormity of what he wants me to do.

"That tree trunk your men brought in this morning, it's a battering ram, right?"

"Yes," Hector says. "We'll load it between the twenty teams. Just before we reach the Greek gates, the horses must be brought to a hard stop."

"And the battering ram will smash into their wall."

"As hard as if one of Zeus' own thunderbolts struck it."

Both of us are staring at the massive tree trunk. It's as long as the stables. The bark has been stripped away and any hint of a branch has been cut and smoothed.

My eyes move to the small seat near the front of the Death Ram. One false move and I'd be thrown off, then be trampled by forty horses' hooves.

"Wren, if we knock down their wall tonight, we stand a chance of ending this war. If we do nothing, we'll starve."

He looks away, hesitating to ask specifically for what I know he wants.

"I need your best horses. And you. No one controls them better, no one guides them with greater skill."

"Who'll lead the charge?" I ask.

"Me. A battalion of my best men will force the Greeks out of the way."

I'm rubbing the palm of my hand over the small center bench that's positioned just above where the battering ram log will be placed. It's too high above the horses, so they'd never hear me clearly. And it's virtually certain that I'd be thrown off when I bring the horses to a hard, fast stop.

"I'll do it, but only if I can saddle Dancer and ride her myself."

His eyes widen with surprise. "That will make it harder to control the reins for the other lead horses. Much harder."

"I'll take that risk."

He looks away. "Wren, don't - "

I cut him off. "I'll prepare the teams."

* * *

Four hundred men, four hundred and forty horses.

And me.

The night air is cold. Each snort and neigh from our stallions spreads a mist into the air that's oddly pretty. Leading the column are brutishly large men with blunt poles, ready to push away anything that tries to stop us.

As the King's Gate closes, the enormity of what we're about to do hits me. I'm shaking a bit, partly because of the cold, partly because I know I might die tonight.

I thought about bringing a shield so that I'll have some protection from the Greek archers, but I can't control the horses and watch for arrows at the same time. The leather chest plate I'm wearing will have to do.

Many battles start with blaring horns and bellowing heralds. Not this one. With the exception of the beating of horses' hooves, our attack will be silent.

We're surrounded by darkness, guided by enemy campfires in the distance instead of a moon. The unending smoke from funeral pyres will make it hard for their lookouts to see us.

"For Soros!" mutters one of the soldiers. Others mumble short prayers before we begin our charge. "For Troy." "For Priam." "For my family!" "For our freedom."

At my request, Hector is tying my belt to Dancer's saddle. I can't risk being thrown off. He's also given me a knife so that I can cut myself loose if I have to.

"Good?" Hector asks me as he pulls on the leather straps around my waist and legs.

"Tighter," I say.

Hector finishes the adjustments, then shouts to the troops, "Say nothing during the charge. Hand signals only!"

Everyone has agreed that our ride will be silent. There will be only two hand signals, and Hector is giving the first one now.

He's at the head of the column. As his sword rises, all see Prince Soros' purple scarf wrapped around the blade. The scarf flutters in the breeze, then flies away. Hector points his sword at the Greek gates and prods his horse.

Our destination is less than a mile away. We've started out with a steady gallop that all of the horses can maintain without much effort.

I fill my lungs with the salty wind blowing off the Aegean Sea. Last night's storm washed the red stains from the beach and the smell of blood from the air. All that will soon change.

We're taking the same path to the battlefield that Prince Soros' soldiers used yesterday. Many of the troops believe that this attack is for revenge.

For me, it's about survival — Troy's survival. And it's for my new family, Hector and Andra.

My father is dead. Mom too. And I may never know whether my twin is alive or covered with blood. All I have left is Hector and Andra.

As we gallop faster, I'm saying their names inside my head as if the words are some kind of incantation: *Hector and Andra, Hector and Andra, Hector and Andra.*

There's no resistance in sight. None of the soldiers remembers the last time a night battle was fought, so the Greeks will definitely be surprised.

Hector increases his speed. We match his pace. I can smell the hog fat from the Greek campfires as we gallop closer and closer.

The enormous log riding atop the Death Ram has been sharpened at the front to a deadly point. Its smooth surface has been greased with fat so that it will slide with maximum speed off the long platform it's mounted on.

I can now see the gates clearly. They're twice as high as our tallest solider. Finally the watchtower sentry sees us.

"Invaders! Archers assemble!"

I hear panic in his voice. It's too late. The wall will be down before a single arrow flies.

There's fear-sweat in the air, but there's also determination. Even if all of us die, what we're about to do will change this war forever.

Hector's fist rises into the air - the final hand signal - and he's punching it into the air. That's exactly what we're going to do to that wall - punch right through it.

The protective column of riders splits away. Hector has done his job.

I'm the leader. It's all up to me.

For this plan to work, I have to push my horses to near stampede speed. I lean forward, one arm cradling my lead horse's neck.

"Fly, Dancer, fly!"

And she strains forward, almost *leaping* with every step.

The Death Ram is rattling, ready to be released. The thundering of horses' hooves is deafening.

Closer, closer! I can't risk failure.

And then I see it – an area already damaged by last night's hellish winds.

I steer Dancer, Dauntless, Ever-strong, and Thunderhoof ever-so-slightly to the left and then scream ...

"HALT!"

I'm pulling back on the reins with everything I have in me.

And the Death Ram shoots toward the wall with shocking speed.

BAM!

A support beam on the wall shatters as if it has been hit by a thunderbolt.

Snap! Snap! Snap!

One, two, *three* timbers are splintered, then pushed aside.

And a section of the wall as wide as twenty chariots crashes to the ground.

Dancer and Ever-Strong are terrified. The roar of battle is never this loud. They're panicking, pulling hard to the left as I'm pulling them back, trying to stop the momentum of forty-horses.

Thunderhoof falls first. Dauntless is next. Helpless, I watch in horror as his head rears up while the ground grows closer. His pleading, terrified eyes meet mine just as I hear his neck break.

"AHHHHH!" I scream. All of my lead horses are down and my left leg is trapped between Dancer and Dauntless.

I pull Hector's knife from my belt and frantically cut the leather straps that are binding me to Dancer's saddle.

"AHHHHH!" Another scream as I pull my leg from between the horses.

"Invaders! Stop the invaders!"

The Greeks weren't ready for this moment. The Trojans were.

The Greek archers, most of them wearing even leather armor, are dying from Trojan arrows.

Flaming arrows are piercing the hull of Agamemnon's ship. From the corner of my eye, I see the timbers, covered with black tar to waterproof them, burst into flame.

"The ships are on fire! The ships are on fire!"

The herald hasn't noticed yet that two sections of the wall are also burning.

I cautiously test my weight on my hurt leg. I can hobble, and that's enough.

The horses are panicking. One by one, I'm cutting them loose from the yolks that are binding them.

Dancer is still down. She's hurt badly, but I'm not giving up on her.

"Can you walk, girl? Can you?!" I pull up on her reins, and to my amazement, she stands.

I lift off her bridle and throw it onto Ever-Strong, then scream in pain as I mount him bareback.

I turn us toward the safety of Priam's fortress-city and flick the reins. Most of my rider-less horses follow.

CHAPTER 16: The Prophecy

NARRATOR: JEM

The Prophecy:
If Greece's bravest slays Troy's boldest,
to Styx he shall swiftly return.

BAM!

First the ground shakes, then I hear the sound of splintering wood and the frantic screaming of the heralds.

"Invaders! Invaders!"

I step from the stables and stare in amazement as soldiers rush to put on their armor.

Soon afterward, I see another sight I barely thought possible: Achilles and Patroclus are arguing.

"If you will not fight, then I must."

"Why?!" Achilles says.

"Agamemnon's ship is on fire. We must drive back the Trojans."

Achilles is unmoved. Stone faced, he asks, "Has our king of kings returned Briseis?"

Patroclus shakes his head.

"Then you know my answer."

Patroclus is near tears. "I've seen ordinary men do extraordinary things simply because they're standing at your side. Your presence inspires them. Let me wear your armor. Let me rally your men!"

"No!"

Patroclus lowers his voice. *"But Hector is at our gates."*

"The man has never wronged me. All who know him say he s an honorable soldier."

"I could stay back from the fighting," Patroclus says softly.

Achilles hesitates. "You give me your word on this?"

Patroclus nods. Achilles opens his tent flap and points at his armor.

I rush into the stables, prepare Achilles' chariot, then hitch four horses to it. One stallion is in the lead position, three others follow. No other warrior uses the same arrangement; no other chariot moves with greater speed.

When I emerge, I see a sight that worries me.

"This is a masquerade!"

Achilles is right. The armor is far too big for Patroclus, so he's wearing a cape over his shoulders to hide his thin shoulders and arms. A few of his golden curls are sticking from the bottom of the helmet.

"But a charade is all we *need*," Patroclus says as he steps into the chariot. "Your men will follow!"

"Which will put you at the forefront of the fighting."

Patroclus leaps into the chariot and sets the stallions in motion, ignoring Achilles' final words. As the horses pass me, I hear Patroclus muttering to himself. "I must be brave, braver than I've ever been."

The words are very unlike my friend, like nothing I've heard him say before.

"Zeus is with us! Achilles has returned!" someone shouts.

The cheering men see only the armor, not the man inside. Perhaps Patroclus is right. Maybe a masquerade is enough.

But his words still haunt me: *Braver than I've ever been.*

An old prophecy flashes through my head:

If Greece's bravest slays Troy's boldest, to Styx he shall swiftly return.

Those who believe in the prophecy say that the day that Achilles slays Hector will mark the beginning of his own end; soon be would be destined to ride atop the waves of the River Styx, which leads to Hades.

Braver than I've ever been. Braver than I've ever been. Braver than I've ever been.

Suddenly dizzy, I lean against one of the hitching posts.

Patroclus is hoping to thwart the prophecy by being Greece's bravest today. If he kills Hector, then Achilles will never have to fight the one man who might defeat him.

I stare at Orion's sword high above me and pray that I'm wrong. But Patroclus' own words tell me I'm right:

I have a life because he gave me a life.

If I ever have the chance to die so that he will live, I'll do it.

I'll never hear his gentle voice again.

* * *

As soldiers churn all around me and horses prance, I climb to the top of the Grecian wooden wall and watch Achilles' black chariot charge toward the center of the battle.

"Achilles!"

The same word is a Grecian battle cry as well as a Trojan call for retreat. A mere suit of armor now has some of the Trojans on the run.

Patroclus is lashing his horses until there's foam flowing past their bridles. The foursome is pulling him with astonishing speed, and the faster they charge, the closer they're moving him toward Hector's sword and spear.

CHAPTER 17: "New stars will fill the night sky."

NARRATOR: WREN

"Wren!" Andra says as I ride through the King's Gate. "I thank the gods that you're still alive. Come, you must eat."

"After the horses are groomed and fed," I shout, then head directly for the stables. Thirty-eight of my forty horses have survived, but I'm not sure that Dancer will live until morning.

I glance at the night sky and immediately see the three stars of Orion's belt. I remember listening to Jem and Homer talk on an evening just like this one.

Oh, how I miss seeing the stars!

Can you see Orion tonight?

Yes, easily.

They say that the greatest warriors are immortalized by Zeus after their final battles. Someday soon, new stars will fill the night sky.

The Greek's barrier wall is on fire; so are several of their ships. Anything can happen tonight, anything!

I'm filled with dread and uncertainty. *Please, please, please, let Jem be safe. Please let Hector live.*

As I'm passing the archery range, I watch as an arrow pierces a straw man that's dressed to look like a Greek warrior.

"... and then a third arrow entered Achilles' black heart."

I recognize the voice immediately: Paris.

He turns to the royal scribe who is often by his side and asks, "Do you like the sound of that – *Achilles' black heart*?"

"I *do*, sire, very much."

Paris sees me and motions me into the archery range. Rolls of papyrus are littered around the scribe's feet.

"Wren, we can tell your tale too, you know!" Paris says exuberantly. "And a thousand years from now, your name, like mine, will still echo throughout the halls of history."

The scribe sees my confusion and explains. "We're writing the history of the Trojan War."

I stare in amazement at Paris. "*You* killed Achilles today?"

"No," he smiles, "but perhaps I will someday."

The scribe hides a smile.

"Surely you realize by now," Paris continues, "that history is written by those with enough gold to hire the best scribes?"

"I ..., I...." For some reason, I always lose my tongue whenever Paris begins spouting his nonsense at me.

"So, young Wren, would you like to be charging into battle atop an all-white stallion or driving a chariot? And how many kills would you like to claim for today?"

"I've got to get to the stables," I say, pointing at the exhausted horses behind me.

Paris laughs, dismisses me with a flick of his skinny wrist, then tells his scribe, "She's been exercising her ponies."

That's when I realize that he has no idea that Hector is fighting for his own life, battling for Troy's survival.

Paris continues his dictation. "Fortified by the love of the world's most beautiful woman, Prince Paris galloped into battle and fought past nightfall. His kills that day numbered forty-five."

"Seventy — let's say seventy, sire."

"Good. Make it so."

I shake my head in wonder. I've never seen Paris leave his walled palace.

It's easier to be brave when your targets don't shoot back.

CHAPTER 18: Forty-Three Spears

<u>NARRATOR: JEM</u>

Achilles is throwing tree branches into an immense pit of fire that's surrounded by stones. The red and orange flames are reflected in the sweat streaming from his chest and back.

The Trojans have been pushed away from our gates, but that's all I know for certain. On the battlefield, the fighting is as loud as I've ever heard it.

I glance up and see a chariot racing toward us. Smoke in the air is making it difficult to see any details.

Achilles notices me staring at the horses. He stops adding branches to the fire.

I squint to verify that one stallion is in the lead position with three other horses following. The chariot is driverless. It's filled with dozens of spears, each poking out at a different angle.

Then I see a leg being dragged through the mud.

As the chariot nears, I realize that the body has not just been stripped of its armor. Naked, it's been stripped of all dignity as well. Each spearhead that pierced the corpse is anchored to the chariot's wooden base, preventing the body from falling into the mud.

The horses come to a halt outside the stables. I force myself to reposition the corpse's shoulders so that we can see the head.

Blond hair. His face is unbloodied, unscarred. Achilles kneels, then touches his dear friend's forehead one last time. His trusted companion since boyhood is gone.

The muscles in his arms and neck become knotted cords. No tears, no wailing, he simply closes his eyes for a moment, inhales deeply, and rises like Poseidon the Earth Shaker from leagues beneath the sea.

"No!" Achilles roars, then strikes some burning logs with an enormous poker, splitting them into pieces.

"No! No! No!"

The horses rear in fright as sparks rise a hundred feet into the coal-black sky.

Throwing the poker aside, Achilles circles the chariot, all the while staring at the many spears and swords that fill the body. But one blade in particular catches his attention. All black, the shaft was rammed from the right side of Patroclus' chest through his left.

It pierced his heart.

The sword's owner shrewdly found Patroclus' weakest point: the gap between the ill-fitting breast plate and the shielding that covered his back.

The black blade is polished obsidian. Nothing is sharper. Only one warrior in the Trojan army uses such a sword.

Achilles can't take his eyes off the elaborately engraved letter on the handle: *H*. His jaw turns to granite as he removes the sword.

"If I must," Achilles says with a bitter snarl, "I'll fight the hounds of Hell to make Hector pay for this."

He turns his gaze toward Troy. "I want your fastest horses, the ones you brought from Lemnos."

Unable to speak, I nod.

"And I need the driver who knows them best. You."

Chills run through me. Hector will die tonight. And so might I.

As Achilles yanks each shaft from Patroclus' body, he's grunting like an animal.

"Forty-three," he mumbles as the last weapon is removed. *"Forty-three* of Hector's men will die tonight. But *he* will be the first."

He points at the still dripping black blade. "Don't clean it. We're taking his filthy sword with us." Achilles pauses. "Do you know where the white phosphorus is hidden?"

I nod.

"Bring it, enough to coat the body. A white burial shroud too."

He stops a herald who's passing by and orders, "Fetch Odysseus. Tell him that I need his help, as well as four pikes."

* * *

Long-pikes were designed for one purpose: to push away enemy ships. But when I return with a burial shroud and the white phosphorus, I see that Ody and Achilles have used the four lengths of iron to transform his chariot.

One of the forty-foot iron shafts has been placed, front-and-center, into a long pipe that extends past the lead-horse's position. An iron pin prevents the pike from slipping out. The tip of its shaft has been sharpened.

I'm even more mystified by what they've done with the other three pikes, which now form a triangular spire that's bolted to the front of the chariot. The spire rises high above and ahead of where the horses will be harnessed.

I've never seen a Greek or Trojan chariot configured in this way.

Achilles is wearing coal-black battle armor used only during night raids. Three Toe told me that Achilles' goddess mother personally asked Vulcan, the god who uses the fires of Hades to forge Zeus' armor, to sculpt the breastplate and shield. I've never seen metal like it.

Bold, Beauty, Black, and Brazen are covered with protective chainmail but aren't yet hitched to the chariot.

Ody, satisfied that his spire of pikes will remain in place on the chariot, walks gravely toward me. He's not in armor. His arms and legs are almost black from the charcoal of the burned timbers inside one of the ships.

"Are you coming with us?" I ask.

He shakes his head.

"You're repairing Agamemnon's ship?"

"No. Tearing it apart." Ody points at the moonless night and the smoke. "Blackness and chaos bring many opportunities, and I, for one, am using them."

His words make no sense. "For?"

"For tomorrow." Ody lowers his voice. "Jem, I have one thing that I must beg of you."

He's never spoken to me using this tone of voice.

"You must come back safely. I need you for my plan."

"A plan?"

He smiles. "Tomorrow we'll fly on the wings of Pegasus over the walls of Troy. And the day after, we'll sail for home."

Before I can open my mouth to ask a thousand questions, he's rushing away.

I carefully lay out the funeral shroud, then try not to look at the horrific wounds all over Patroclus' cold corpse. When we finish wrapping it inside the white cloak, it looks like a cocoon.

Wordlessly, Achilles lifts the body onto his left shoulder and steps onto a pile of hay bails stacked four-high. After tying the shroud to the pikes with seven leather straps, we double-coat it with white phosphorus.

Satisfied with our work, Achilles steps down, then dangles the end of a cloth into our campfire. I curl my arms around Bold's neck as Achilles hurls the burning rag onto the highest point of the triangular pike spire.

"Easy, girl, easy," I whisper, but even I'm startled as the shroud bursts into flames.

"And so it begins," Achilles says to himself.

The beginning of what? His destiny? His mother's prophecy? The beginning of the end of this horrible war?

I slip on a leather chest protector, then step into the chariot and take the reins. Silently, stoically, Achilles joins me.

* * *

Word has spread among the elite Spartan warriors. The man they've sworn to die for will fight again. They now encircle our campfire. Each is in full battle armor. All carry a spear, a sword, and a shield.

Thump-thump, *clang!*

A single Spartan warrior begins the ritual rhythm that announces a major battle, one that might decide the outcome of a war.

Hundreds more join in: two thumps of the base of their spears against the rocks underfoot are followed by an incredibly loud clang as the shafts strike their shields.

The sounds reverberate inside my chest. I'm fighting to keep my emotions from overwhelming me, but there's no question that I'm part of something that's monumental, something world-changing.

"Men of honor, assemble!" shouts the sentry.

Many of the warriors who are joining us are still recovering from serious wounds. Strips of blood-drenched bandages can be seen underneath their dark armor. It's as if Hell has vomited the living-dead onto the battlefield to confront the Trojans.

Three hundred horses and riders are now following our chariot.

High above us, Patroclus' shroud is burning with incredible brightness. A leather strap around his right wrist gives way and an arm falls. His hand is now pointing directly at the heart of Priam's walled city.

Achilles' voice thunders across the plain.

"Hector! Behold Flaming Death! He comes for *you."*

Brazen lunges ahead. Soon more than a thousand hooves are thundering along a path that leads only to Troy.

To the men in Hector's legion, it must look as if the Grim Reaper in his black armor is being pulled by the four horses of the apocalypse. Patroclus' fiery body is a demon from the underworld flying toward them.

CHAPTER 19: "The next few hours will decide this war."

NARRATOR: WREN

I wake up moaning. My left leg is horribly bruised and swollen.

After grooming and feeding the horses, I allowed myself to rest against a stack of hay. Either I passed out or else succumbed to exhaustion.

As I shake the haze from my head, I hear Hector's voice near the stable entrance. He's praying.

"Athena, grant me wisdom. Apollo, help me push past pain. I ask for no glory and I beg for no man's life, including my own. But I pray that you'll protect my wife, my child, and our dear Wren."

I allow him a few moments of privacy, then limp past a hundred hanging bridles.

I'm shocked at his appearance. Every inch of his body is splattered with blood, most of it from his enemies, some of it, his own.

"You're going back out there?!" I say.

"Yes. I need a chariot and fresh horses."

"Don't, *please*. You're wounded."

"The next few hours will decide this war."

I see the determination in his eyes, then grab the chainmail that will protect Ever-Strong and Thunderhoof from arrows and spears.

"The Greek ships are on fire," Hector tells me as we harness the horses to his chariot. Soon they'll have no way home."

"They're desperate. That's good, right?"

He shakes his head. "Desperate men do desperate things. And they fight as if they have nothing to lose."

He kneels and begins untying his war spoils, some truly magnificent armor. Then he turns over the chest plate and I realize that I've already seen its golden phoenix rising from the flames.

"Achilles."

"No. An imposter was wearing his armor. I suspect he'll be coming soon to get it back."

"What about the legend, the one that says that Achilles was dipped in the River Styx and can't be killed?"

"It's an old myth, nothing more. All men have weaknesses, and so far I've been blessed to always find them. And the Styx runs like white-water rapids from beginning to end, so a baby would be washed away in an instant."

"Maybe his mother held him by his heels?"

"See?" he says reassuringly. "Everyone has a weakness. And besides," he startles me by striking Achilles' armor with his sword, "I've never been better protected." The armor is still shining, unscratched.

Hector doesn't know what I know. He hasn't seen what I've seen. If there's one man who can kill him, it's Achilles.

I've *got* to stop him from going onto that battlefield.

"There's something I haven't told you."

Hector finishes putting on the last piece of Achilles' armor, then turns. He's giving me his complete attention.

"I have a twin. The Greeks might force him to drive one of their chariots tonight." Tears begin flowing down my face. "His name is Jem. Please don't kill him."

Hector bends onto one knee and looks me in the eye. "If the gods allow me to live tonight, Jem will join our home. I will be as much a father to him as I am to you."

"I'm begging you. Don't go."

"I must."

I wipe away my tears. "Then I must be your driver, no one else."

NARRATOR: JEM

As we race toward Troy, the grim reality of this battle chills me. The sands are once again saturated with blood. Corpses are scattered everywhere, most of them Greek.

But thousands, not just hundreds, might die during the next few hours. And tonight we'll learn whether or not Achilles is truly immortal.

Faster and faster we gallop, and soon I can smell the smoke from the animal fat that fuels many of the Trojan torches. As we approach the walled city, I watch a squadron of archers rush to the highest battlements. The main gates of Priam's fortress groan in protest as they're opened widely.

Hector's chariot leads the others. His color guard follows. All purple, the crown-prince's elite forces are with him tonight.

A huge H covers the front of his chariot.

"Keep us steady, Jem. Point us toward the center of that royal crest."

Achilles leans forward toward the iron chassis. He pulls a metal ring attached to a pin, then braces himself.

"Halt!"

I pull the reins back, hard and tight. Brazen, Beauty, Black, and Bold stop abruptly, but the sharpened pike hurtles forward ...

... and pierces the H on the crest. Enraged, Hector leaps from the chariot as his driver falls onto the battlefield.

My eyes widen.

"Wren!" I scream.

She's not moving. Two spear-throws separate us.

Hector's jaw hardens as he stands alone, unafraid. He's wearing a breastplate I recognize immediately: it's from the armor he stripped off of Patroclus' body.

"Stay down." Achilles pushes me to the floor of our chariot and leaps from it.

I ignore his order, flick the reins ever-so-slightly, and inch the horses toward my twin.

Achilles lifts his sword high above his head, then slowly points it at Hector.

It's a challenge: one man against the other, no one else.

And Hector nods.

CHAPTER 20: "Then take it!"

NARRATOR: WREN

I shake the dirt and sand from my hair, then try to stand. As soon as I put pressure on my left leg, it screams at me. The fall from the chariot has made it worse.

"Stay in the chariot. You'll be safe there," Hector says quietly to me, then pulls an enormous pike from the metal crest and balances it in his right hand. His arm muscles tense.

"Thanks for the *gift*," Hector shouts at Achilles, then releases the "spear" with catapult force.

I'm as amazed as Hector is when it shatters against Achilles' black shield. Both men are protected by armor forged in the intense heat of the Underworld.

"You're not worthy of that armor!" Achilles roars. "It's mine."

"Then take it!" Hector says. He widens his stance and stands his ground.

Achilles begins his charge. I've seen the bursts of speed he's capable of, but today he's sprinting toward *me*, and I'm terrified.

The clanging of one god-forged sword against another shocks me back to alertness. The sound is like a thunderclap.

Hector's on one knee but quickly recovers.

Blam! Blam! Blam!

Their shields collide as Achilles tries to push Hector to the ground, but Hector deflects the blow and steps aside, forcing Achilles to be off balance for a heartbeat or two. I've seen him briefly outmaneuvered when attacked by six men, but never by one.

Achilles charges again, but this time he leaps so that he's positioned at least three feet above Hector, an angle that gives his sword a clear path between the base of Hector's neck and the unprotected area next to his collar bone.

Hector sees the blade, rolls, then springs to his feet, unbloodied.

Achilles is down. Sandy mud covers his hands and the armor over his knees. Breathing heavily, he rises.

"You are a worthy opponent," Achilles says, "but you'll die like all the rest."

"You sent an unworthy *boy* in a god's armor to kill me." There's no fear in Hector's voice. "His blood is on your hands, not mine."

They're taunting each other, each hoping that the other will make a hotheaded mistake.

Part of me wants to watch. Another part wants to look away. Someone I love is going to die today.

Out of the corner of my eye, I see something moving. Achilles' chariot is creeping toward me. The driver is crouched down, barely visible. Then I see his eyes.

Jem.

My brother gulps, then nods. Both of us are protected by our chariots, but that situation will change quickly as soon as either Hector or Achilles dies. The Greek and Trojan soldiers have separated so that they can witness this battle.

After the victor strips the other's armor, Jem and I will be caught in a vice as the two armies rage against each other.

Hector's horses neigh. They're afraid of the burning corpse that's moving closer and closer to them.

I wedge myself between Thunderhoof and Ever-Strong. "It's okay; I'm here," I coo to them.

As always, Brazen leads Achilles' horses.

"Halt," I command, and my beloved Brazen obeys. He has not forgotten me.

Hector now has a sword in one hand, a spear in the other. He charges.

CLANG!

Their blades meet – again and again and again. Then Achilles' sword falls to the ground.

From a scabbard on his right side, Achilles draws a bloodied black sword. I gasp as I see the letter H on the handle.

He begins twisting and turning while the black blade cuts through the wind. A chill runs through me.

With the precision of a surgeon, Achilles angles the sword so that it slices through one of the leather ties that connects Hector's chest-plate to the armor covering his back.

Hector's eyes flair. He knows he's vulnerable.

Achilles flings the obsidian blade into the air, then spins to reposition himself. The shaft is now horizontal to the ground.

Achilles seizes the shaft with his right hand and holds it as if it's a spear. With barely a heartbeat's hesitation, he hurls the black blade at the unprotected flesh on Hector's left side.

The opening is no wider than a fingertip.

But the blade pierces Hector's chest and does not stop until it reaches the armor on the other side. My protector thuds to the ground.

"Get up!" roar the Trojans, "Get up!"

The archers on the fortress walls are shouting mindlessly, somehow believing that the impossible will be possible.

Achilles turns to face Patroclus' still-burning body, then cuts the ties that hold the corpse to the spire.

The shroud falls a spear's length from Hector's body.

Achilles kneels, closes his eyes, and says simply, 'I have avenged you, my friend. Walk tall in the Underworld."

I can feel the heat from the white phosphorus. And seemingly so can Hector. To my amazement, he somehow lifts himself onto his left elbow. His spear is still in his right hand.

He dips the tip into the white fire from Hell, then focuses on the still kneeling Achilles.

His half-dead eyes widen as he mutters, "She held him by his heel!"

And the flaming spear flashes through the night and pierces its target.

Achilles' cry fills the battlefield. It's like nothing I've heard before.

His jaws almost unhinge as he screams the scream of a half-man/half-god who finally understands what unbearable pain feels like.

But there's something else etched onto his face that I don't understand. Surprise.

And that's when I realize: he didn't know about his only weakness. And neither did Thetis, his mother. If she'd known, she would have told him, would have provided armor for her son that protected the only patch of skin on his body where Death could enter.

Achilles is crawling, moving toward Hector, then his head falls to the sandy soil.

Hector's eyes close first. Then Achilles'.

Like the ultimate warrior, Hector somehow found the strength to kill his own killer.

Jem's eyes meet mine. Both of our protectors are now dead, taken from us by this awful war.

From the walls of Troy I hear, "Archers, strike!" I recognize the commander's voice: Paris, Hector's unworthy brother. His bow is the first to unleash an arrow.

I watch carefully as it flies toward us, then see the shaft bounce from Achilles' armor. A hundred arrows follow. Some of them pierce his hands and legs. I turn away and force myself to remember that nothing can hurt him again.

There's no doubt in my mind that Paris' lying tongue will claim the kill. He knows I'm down here, yet he's ordered the strike. To him, I'm nothing.

"Wren! Come here!" Jem shouts.

I shake my head. "I'm hurt! And I have no shield!"

The look on his face terrifies me. I've seen it before: he's paralyzed by fear.

"Help me!" I scream. "Get Achilles' shield."

His arm darts out, then returns to the safety of his chariot. He's trembling.

"You've got to do this!" I shout.

Or we'll both die.

As arrows fly overhead, Jem grabs Achilles' shield, ducks under it, and begins crawling toward me.

Thump! Thump! Thump! Arrows hit the shield and bounce off.

Finally he reaches me. "Get under the shield. There's room for both of us."

My left leg is almost worthless, but somehow we drag ourselves to Achilles' chariot.

"We've *got* to get back to the tents," Jem whispers. "Ody has a plan."

"To do what?"

"To take us home."

With the shield covering our backs, Jem rises. He grabs the reins and shouts a command that our lead horse knows well.

"Fly, Brazen, fly!"

CHAPTER 21: Pegasus

NARRATOR: WREN

As I awaken, I remember the final words that Ody spoke before I closed my eyes last night.

If you're a wolf and you want a flock of sheep to invite you to dinner, first you must disguise yourself, then tempt them with a pretty package.

Jem, I, Ody, Three Toe, and Two Blade are inside "the pretty package." We're on the shores once lined by hundreds of Grecian ships. Only two huge structures remain: the burnt remains of Agamemnon's ship and the wooden winged horse we're hiding in.

The other ships sailed not for Greece, but to Tenedos, a cove along the coast no more than an hour's sail away. Everything depends on a weasel named Dolon, a Trojan who'd sell his soul for seventeen silvers. Ody paid the man, in advance, two gold bars for the one simple thing he must do for us today.

But *will* he do it?

Two gold bars?! said Three Toe. *For that, I'd run naked past Priam's palace.*

When I buy a man, Ody answered, *I want him to stay bought.*

If Dolon is loyal to Ody, he's betraying Troy. But if he betrays us, the Trojans will make him a hero, a very, very rich hero.

And the five of us will be dead.

I force myself to think about something besides failure: Pegasus. A hundred men worked throughout the night to build this amazing horse.

Ody prides himself on knowing each soldier's talents, and somehow he remembered that a man named Epeios – a truly pathetic cook and an even worse soldier – was a master with his hands, a carpenter who could construct almost anything.

And this horse – Pegasus – that we're hiding inside is his finest creation.

Ten men high and a spear's throw in length, it's a jaw-dropping sight from afar. And the closer Jem and I came to it, the more impressed we were.

Each of its four wheels is taller than a man. As the axles turn, Pegasus' wings and tail move as well. It's grey stone eyes, like Athena's, seem filled with wisdom and mystery.

All of its wood, blackened by smoke from last night's fire, was salvaged from the timbers of Agamemnon's ship.

The Trojans awoke to the sight of Athena's favorite black stallion, Pegasus, waiting for them on the white sands in front of the King's Gate. It looks like a gift from the gods, a long-awaited present congratulating them on their defeat of the Greeks.

And as the morning light crept inside Epeios' gift to us, we marveled at the ingeniousness of his design. I'm crammed inside the left wing; Three Toe's in the right one. Whale blubber was needed to grease up Two Blade so that he'd fit into the tail. Ody's in the head. Jem's inside the lower jaw.

Only one of us, Jem, has a forked hammer that will remove the pegs sealing us inside. Once the wooden plugs within Pegasus' mouth are pried loose, the jaws will drop and we'll lower a rope ladder.

But first, Dolon will have to give his little speech, the one that he and Ody practiced over and again last night. I'm praying he hasn't overslept.

Hundreds of astonished people are pouring from Troy's gates. Their voices are growing louder.

"Only the gods could have built such a wonder."

"Its eyes are like Athena's. It's her gift to us."

"But why is the horse staring at the *sea*, not Troy?!"

"Burn it!" screams a woman. "This black demon is from Hades."

My heart is racing. If they start a fire, we'll never escape in time.

"What you see is no gift from the gods. I, Laocoon, Apollo's priest, promise you that, citizens of Troy. This horse holds Troy's downfall!"

"How?!"

The crowd becomes hushed. The man spoke only one word, but I'd know his voice anywhere: Paris.

He repeats the question. "How, venerable priest, do you know that this winged wonder contains evil?"

The priest is silent.

"Let's look inside," Paris says to the crowd.

THUD!

A spear enters the horse's side. I hear the sound of splintering wood as its bronze blade pries a board loose. Then another.

A wheel creaks as someone climbs the spokes toward the horse's belly. Now he's poking a spear inside – left, right, up, and down.

"Join me, soothsayer," Paris shouts to the priest, "and we'll peer inside together."

The wheel groans again as the priest ascends.

"I see nothing," he says, "but my prophecy remains. This horse will be our undoing!"

Another voice joins the crowd.

"I saw the bastards roll this giant onto our shores!"

Dolon. But his words are not the ones I heard rehearsed last night.

"I hate the Greeks, we all do!" he shouts. "They're butchers. So trust me when I tell you what I saw from the shadows."

If he betrays us, we'll soon be dead.

"The Greeks knelt and prayed before this statue last night!" Dolon continues. "They believe that Poseidon himself can see its shining eyes from the bottom of the ocean. They pleaded with him to smooth the seas for them for as long as this tribute remains on the shore."

I breathe a sigh of relief. I heard Ody say each of those words, then Dolon.

The crowd is pushing Pegasus so that his eyes shine on Troy, not the sea.

"Poseidon, sink their ships!" someone screams over and over. Others pick up the chant.

"Take the horse inside the gates!" shouts another.

Yes! We're going inside the walled city that has defeated all attackers for a hundred years.

"I, Prince Paris, the man who sent Achilles to the Underworld, declare this to be a day of feasting and celebration! Let us rejoice!"

* * *

Hour after hour, the dancing and revelry continue. Paris has given the same speech three times:

My iron-tipped arrows showed Achilles what Trojans are made of! Poseidon will send the Greeks to a watery grave! Drink! Rejoice!

Each time he speaks, he slurs his words more.

Long past midnight, Jem removes two simple wooden pegs. Pegasus' lower jaw drops. The courtyard's cobblestones are sixty feet below.

"What do you see?" Ody whispers. He's still inside Pegasus' head.

"A guard."

Before we lower the rope ladder and crawl from the horse's mouth, someone has to knock that guard senseless. And only one of us has a chance of doing that before we're on the ground.

"Get Three Toe," Ody says to Jem.

Until this moment, I have not been thankful that we have a slinger as part of our crew. I've been listening for hours to the low rumble of his snoring.

Cautiously, quietly, Jem crawls toward Pegasus' right wing.

"Wake up," Jem says as he tap-tap-taps on a wing joint.

"Go away," mumbles Three Toe.

"It's time to work," Jem tells him.

Using a forked hammer that's tied to his belt – Ody was afraid Jem would drop it inside the horse's dark belly – my twin removes the five pegs that are keeping a large wooden panel in place.

Because of those panels, we were unseen even after Paris and Laocoon stared inside Pegasus.

Three Toe crawls from the right wing, guided only by the sliver of moonlight that's streaming through the horse's jaws. They free me next by pulling my shoulders from the left wing.

"How's your leg?" Jem whispers.

"A little better."

I know I can limp, but I'll fall if I try to run. That fact worries me a lot.

Jem's next stop is Pegasus' tail, where Two Blade and his double-edged ax have been hiding. And finally we release Ody from the head.

Each of us struggles toward the horse's open jaws, then stares down at the courtyard. It's Troy's main square where many of the city's residents meet before going to the surrounding shops.

"Four torches," Ody says, pointing at the bronze posts that mark the north, east, south, and west corners of the square. Pegasus is in the center.

The guard on duty rises from the boulder he's been sitting on and walks the perimeter. He's unsteady on his feet, perhaps because he's groggy or, more likely, he enjoyed the wine that was being shared by almost everyone during the day-long celebration.

"*Please* don't look up," I mutter softly. If he notices that the horse's jaws are now open, we're dead.

Three Toe crawls until his head and right arm are hanging out of Pegasus' mouth.

"Jem, load my sling." Three Toe says.

There's no position that's comfortable and no room for Three Toe to maneuver. Jem cautiously hands the loaded leather slingshot to him.

But the lead ball falls, then bounce-bounce-bounces across the courtyard's cobblestones.

I hold my breath.

The guard turns slowly, searching for a dog or rabbit that might have set a pebble in motion.

Thankfully, he does not look up.

The guard presses his cupped fingers to his lips and blows warm air over them. He's just as cold as we are. He sits, then crosses his arms over his chest for warmth.

"Wait," Ody says as Jem loads another lead ball into Three-Toe's sling.

The guard's head slumps forward and his breathing becomes very regular.

"Now!"

Three Toe spins the two-string sling, increases the speed, squints, and releases one end.

It whizzes past its target, missing by two feet.

"Damn!" Three Toe mutters.

The guard snorts, looks around, then stands.

"Triple ball, hurry!"

Jem loads the three lead rocks, Three Toe launches them.

Bam! Bam! Bam!

The first ball connects with the guard's right shoulder, the second with his thick neck, and the third with the side of his head. As he falls, his right temple strikes the boulder.

That's one Trojan who won't be troubling us before sunrise.

Three Toe releases the rope ladder. All
of us move back as he awkwardly tries to
reposition his rather large butt so that
it's dangling from the horse's mouth.

"Careful," Ody cautions. "The fall will
kill you."

Three Toe's back end is high above the
cobblestones. He lowers his right leg,
anchors his foot on one of the rope
rungs, and begins his descent. The rope
ladder swings left to right, then right
to left with each footstep.

Ody is next. Two Blade follows.

"Toss me my ax, handle first!"

Jem does the tossing. Two Blade does the
catching. No blood is shed.

"You're next," Jem tells me. "I'll hold
your arm, just in case."

Just in case your leg gives out.

My body was twisted inside Pegasus' left
wing for many hours. Now I'm asking it
to make precise movements. My bruised
left leg is screaming at me.

Ody climbs toward me as I start my
descent.

"We can do this," he reassures me, then wraps both arms around me. My father, a strong yet tender man, could do no finer job.

Inch by inch, step by step – somehow we make it down.

Jem is last. As soon as his feet touch the cobblestones, Ody grabs two torches, hands one to Three Toe, then begins rattling off orders.

"We'll separate into two teams. Three Toe and Two Blade, do what you must to get to the West Gate. Use the darkest alley ways. Half of the Spartans in our army are waiting for you to let them in. Jem, Wren, and I will open the King's Gate. If we succeed, then tonight marks the last day of this war."

We separate.

Ody's right. The Trojans have nothing to match the Spartans' speed and skill – or their brutality.

And that's what troubles me. Hector and Andra were good to me, trusted me. I can't live with myself if I allow the Spartans and their always-lethal swords into the palace.

Andra and her son must survive.

As I limp across the courtyard, I'm fighting back tears.

"I can't run. And I can't fight. I'm sorry."

Ody kneels, then forces me to look into his kind eyes. "No one on this team is more valuable than you are."

Surely he's lying. Everyone knows he's good at it.

"You can still ride?" he asks.

"Of course," I say.

"Can you help us find horses, strong ones?"

I nod.

"And do you know where the Trojans buy their lamp oil?"

"Yes."

"No one else knows all those things," Ody whispers to me. "Lamp oil first."

Jem states the obvious. "We don't have a lamp."

Ody nods. "We don't need one, just the oil. We're going to start two fires. Big ones."

Seconds later, I'm riding on his strong back as I lead him through alleyways to the agora where at least two of the merchants will have what we need.

"To the right," I say. "It's the shop with the whitewashed door."

Jem tests the latch on the off chance that the shop owner forgot to bar his door tonight. "Locked."

Ody shrugs. "His sloppy carpenter has already opened it for us."

Ody kneels and I slide off his back. His fingernails find a rough edge on one of the door panels, and he begins tugging. A large square of wood falls into his hands.

"Think you can make it through?" Ody whispers.

Jem nods.

"The lamp oil is on the right," I tell him, "but be careful. The owner sleeps in the back."

Jem's face turns pale. Then he crawls through.

I hold my breath and listen as he makes each step.

Ker-plunk.

Ody's eyes widen.

"*Brooms*," I say, "he also sells brooms!"

"I'll slit yer throat yah clumsy little thief!"

Ody reaches past the open panel, throws the door-bar to the floor, and rushes inside.

"Not today," says Ody, almost calmly. Vice-like, his hand surrounds the man's wrist. A knife falls into a pile of brooms. Moments later, the shop owner's neck is inside the V-shaped crook of Ody's arm. The heavy man struggles, then goes slack as Ody increases the pressure on the throbbing blood vessel in his neck.

"Get some sleep," Ody says to the man. "And thanks for the knife."

I'm wild-eyed with fear. "Hurry!" I say to Jem as I point our torch at the amphorae that hold lamp oil.

"There's no need to rush," says Ody. He reaches into the pouch attached to his belt, removes three silvers, and places them into the shopkeeper's open hand. After a moment's hesitation, he adds two more coins.

Seeing my disbelieving eyes, he says, "For the oil. And the door."

Jem, an amphora in each arm, steps outside first, then I mount Ody's back. As we leave, Ody closes the door as if we're normal customers who have made some late night purchases.

"Where are large celebrations held?" Ody asks me.

"The amphitheater."

"All stone?"

I nod.

"Are there wooden buildings nearby?"

"There's a large tent next to it that was set up for Prince Soros' funeral. There's lots of straw inside it."

"Perfect. Where?"

I'm the rider, he's my well-trained horse. The slightest movement of my head or arms sends him galloping in the right direction.

We check inside the unguarded tent, then Jem empties one of the amphora onto the straw and the coiled hemp ropes. Our torch ignites the blaze, and soon flames are rising high into the night sky.

"Half the guards in the city will soon be fighting this fire," Ody says. "Now we're going to attract the other half."

Jem's eyebrows rise to the top of his head.

"The horse," Ody explains.

We rush unseen from one back alley to another, then arrive at our destination. The guard is still unconscious and the goose egg on his head has grown considerably.

Ody climbs the spokes of one of the wheels, spreads the lamp oil along Pegasus' legs and belly, then lights it. The horse is such a work of art that I hate to see it destroyed.

The King's Gate is in sight. A guard comes running to put out the blaze.

We retreat to a backstreet.

"Hide here," Ody tells us.

When he returns, he's wearing the guard's uniform.

"And now we're going to open the gate. There's still one man on duty there and I'll need your help – both of you."

My heart is pounding as we sneak from shadow to shadow. Ody whispers something in Jem's ear, then disappears into the night.

"Play dead," Jem says softly.

"Help! My sister's been hurt!" he shouts.

The guard is suspicious. "Bring her here!"

Jem shakes his head. "I can't. She's been burned!"

Ody is creeping behind the man, as unseen as a black panther.

"Help us!" Jem pleads.

When I look up again, the guard is on the ground, struggling against a gag and his own belt, which now binds his hands behind him.

"Jem - quickly!" Ody motions us toward the gate.

He yokes one of the oxen, Jem the other. Then the two beasts perform the only duty they've probably ever had: opening the King's Gate.

The huge wooden beams groan and the two halves gradually separate. Ody walks to the center of the gate with a torch in hand.

He stands tall, then moves his torch in a huge circle. Then another. He turns toward the burning horse and slashes the night sky with the torch's flame.

The men from Achilles' elite Spartan troops have been waiting for this signal. The first O means that Ody is the signaler. The second indicates that the King's Gate is open. The rapid slash means that the Greeks can charge inside with little resistance.

Not long after, we hear the thudding of boots against cobblestones coming from the opposite direction. Hundreds of warriors are running in sync: a Spartan signature.

"Three Toe and Two Blade — they did it!" Jem says.

Ody nods.

The two main entrances to this city are now open. Troy's fate has been sealed.

Ody glances at my face. "What's wrong?"

"Hector and his wife," I explain, "were kind to me. They have a baby. Please don't ...." My voice trails off. I can't bear to say the words.

Ody pulls me closer. "And their kindness will be repaid. You have my word."

I nod, more grateful than I can express.

"The king's stables — are they near?" he asks me. There's urgency in his voice.

"Yes."

And once again I'm atop Ody's back with Jem at our side. As we near the royal compound, Ody enters the shadows. I can see the guard but he can't see us.

"Do you know him?" Ody whispers.

"Yes."

"Good. I'm guessing that all of the guards know each other. Is that true?"

"They're friends," I say. "He'll know you're not one of them as soon as he sees your face, but the uniform you're wearing will get us close enough."

Ody's eyebrows rise. "You have a plan?"

"Half of one."

He smiles. "That's a good start."

"Carry Jem and me in your arms. My hair will hide your face. We'll both look hurt. Then I'll tell the guard about the fire."

"And I won't need to say a word," Ody says.

I nod.

"I could moan," Jem says, "or act like I'm dying."

Ody looks him firmly in the eye. "Don't over do it."

Ody pushes his helmet as low as possible over his forehead, positions Jem over his left shoulder, and gathers me into his arms.

We emerge from the shadows.

And Jem begins moaning as if his guts are falling out. Thankfully, the guard recognizes me immediately.

"Wren!" he says, "Andra has been worried about you!"

I ignore his comment and say breathlessly, "Marcus and Theos need your help! There's a fire at the amphitheater."

Our ruse works!

Moments later, we're in the stables.

"Which are your best runners?" Ody asks.

I point. "Thunderhoof, Ever-Strong, Dauntless ... and Moonshadow."

The white-maned mare is Andra's favorite.

I lean against one of the stalls so that all of my weight is on my good leg. Jem brings me bridles as Ody selects saddles. Despite the unusual hour, the horses accept the bits in their mouths without complaint.

"Where are the royal bedchambers?" Ody asks as we leave the stables.

I point and we make our way upstairs. Fear and doubt are written all over Jem's face.

"Wren, this is dangerous," he says. "There'll be more guards. The horses are saddled; we should go – *now*."

I shake my head. "If you and Ody want to stay in the stables, you can. I *have* to do this."

Ody touches Jem's shoulder. "These people know and trust Wren," Ody says. "And this is a moment when we need to trust her. Okay?"

Jem nods.

"Good," Ody says, then picks me up and climbs the stairs wordlessly.

Cautiously, I peer around a corner and sigh with relief that the corridor is empty.

"Wait here," I say, "I've got to do the rest of this on my own."

"You're sure?" Ody asks.

I nod.

Limping badly, I enter the nursery, then lift Hector and Andra's son into my arms. He whimpers only for a moment. Andra's bedroom is next door.

"Who's there?!" she calls out.

"Me, Wren."

"Wren! I thank the gods that you're safe."

"I ... I - "

"What's wrong?" Andra says as she enters the nursery.

"The gates are open. Troy is being attacked."

"Surely we're safe here."

I shake my head. "The guards are fighting two large fires."

She quickly lights a lamp and looks me in the eye. "You've been gone for more than a day. Is there something you're not telling me?" There's suspicion in her voice.

I point at the shadow in the hallway. "There's a man here who can get us past the Greek troops."

Torch in hand, Ody shows his face.

"You are not one of our guards!"

Ody surprises me by bowing. In a voice just above a whisper, he says, "I am Odysseus of Ithaca."

Andra gasps. "Every officer in our army knows your name! Your loyalty is to Agamemnon."

"No longer," Ody says. "The war is over. Troy's gates are burning and the Spartans control them."

Andra's face is full of anger and confusion. "Who let you in?!"

"Paris," Ody says. "The moment he wheeled the wooden horse inside the gates, he sealed Troy's fate. I will help you and your son find a safe place outside these walls, but first you must decide who to trust, Wren or Paris."

Andra glances at her son in my arms, then at Ody. "Priam is dead?"

Ody shakes his head. "Not yet. He'll be held as a hostage."

Her mouth hardens. "Our king will kill himself before he'll allow Agamemnon to use him as a bargaining chip."

"I agree," Ody says. "And that is why you must decide who to follow tonight. On your command, we'll leave your palace immediately."

She hesitates. "Would I be a slave in Greece?"

"Never," Ody says.

"One more question before I trust you with my son's life."

Ody nods.

"How can you fight for Agamemnon, a pig of a man?"

"I, too, have a son," Ody begins.

There's a tremor of emotion in his voice that I've never heard before.

"And when Agamemnon asked me to join his unjust war, I refused."

"But you're here," Andra says bitterly.

Ody nods. "He took me aside and promised me that my wife and son would one day die mysteriously because I refused to add my troops to his. Today he has his victory. I'm free."

Andra stands. "We must hurry."

Ody nods. "We'll wait in the hallway while you dress."

Soon the woman who should have been at Hector's side as he ruled Troy joins us. She's wearing her maid's clothes. Andra takes her baby from my arms and follows us to the stables.

She sees Moonshadow already saddled and turns to me. "Bless you."

We mount our horses. Jem catches Ody's eye and asks, "Where are we going?"

His answer is simple.

"Home."

BOOKS BY LEE SMYTH

For the latest Lee Smyth novels, go to **www.LeeSmyth.com**

Books in the **Take-It-to-the-_MAX_ series** for video-game fanatics can be read in any order, but the following sequence is recommended: 1. MAX RoW (Righters of Wrongs), 2. MAX CoW (Crazies of Wahoo), 3. MAX WoW (World of Wheels), 4. MAX PoW (Prom of Wahoo).

In the **GoG series (Gods of Games)** for video-game addicts, _Total Control_ and _Total O.P.M._ are for teens and are best when read in that order.

Total Catastrophe, Totally Unleashed, and _Total Chaos_ can be read in any order and are recommended for both middle schoolers & teens. Animal lovers will LOVE _Totally Unleashed_ and _Total Catastrophe_ (which is also known as "Total Cat").

Books in the **WARRIORS series** can be read in any order: 1. Achilles' Rage, 2. Tel's Odyssey, 3. (planned) Hercules' Pain.

Books in the **Mac and Dekker series** ("James Bond" for a new generation of readers) can be read in any order, but the following sequence is recommended: 1. Midas, 2. Shoot the Moon, 3. (planned) The Big Bang.

Books in the **Re-Imagined series** can be read in any order: 1. Treasure Island (a re-imagining of Robert Louis Stevenson's Treasure Island), 2. Frankenstein, My Father (a re-imagining of Mary Shelley's Frankenstein), 3. White Scar, the Ship Wrecker (a re-imagining of Herman Melville's Moby Dick).

OTHER NOVELS for teens by Lee Smyth: 1. Rev Willie, A Voodoo-Hoodoo Gumbo, With Blood (And Laughs), 2. Damaged, 3. Filthy Rich + Dirt Poor. For details, see **www.LeeSmyth.com**

If you liked this novel, Lee would be grateful if you'd rate it five-stars on Amazon.com.

Visit Lee's website at **www.LeeSmyth.com**

Made in the USA
Las Vegas, NV
08 December 2022